THE

BIG

EMPTY

D0029871

THE
BIG
EMPTY

BY
J.B. STEPHENS

SAN DIEGO PUBLIC LIBRARY
TEEN SERVICES

3 1336 07263 6807

razOr
bill
NEW YORK

The Big Empty

RAZORBILL

Published by the Penguin Group
Penguin Young Readers Group
345 Hudson Street, New York, New York 10014, U.S.A.
Penguin Group (USA) Inc., 375 Hudson Street, New York, New York 10014, U.S.A
Penguin Books Canada Ltd, 10 Alcorn Avenue, Toronto, Ontario, Canada M4V 3B2 (a
division of Pearson Penguin Canada, Inc.)
Penguin Books Ltd, 80 Strand, London WC2R 0RL, England
Penguin Ireland, 25 St Stephen's Green, Dublin 2, Ireland
(a division of Penguin Books Ltd)
Penguin Group (Australia), 250 Camberwell Road, Camberwell, Victoria 3124, Australia
(a division of Pearson Australia Group Pty Ltd)
Penguin Books India Pvt Ltd, 11 Community Centre, Panchsheel Park,
New Delhi – 110 017, India
Penguin Group (NZ), Cnr Airborne and Rosedale Roads, Albany, Auckland, New Zealand
(a division of Pearson New Zealand Ltd)
Penguin Books (South Africa) (Pty) Ltd, 24 Sturdee Avenue, Rosebank, Johannesburg
2196, South Africa

Penguin Books Ltd, Registered Offices: 80 Strand, London WC2R 0RL, England

10 9 8 7 6 5 4 3 2 1

Copyright © 2004 By George Productions, Inc. and Amy Garvey
All rights reserved

Interior design by Christopher Grassi

Library of Congress Cataloging-in-Publication Data
Stephens, J. B.
  The Big Empty / by J.B. Stephens.
    p. cm. — (The Big Empty ; 1)
  Summary: After half of the world's population is killed by a plague, seven teenagers seek
a better life in a nightmarish future by deciphering coded messages and trying to avoid
the Slashers.
  ISBN 1-59514-006-9 (pbk.)
  [1. Survival—Fiction. 2. Science fiction.] I. Title. II. Series: Stephens, J. B. Big Empty ;
v 1.
  PZ7.S83214Bi 2004
  [Fic]—dc22

                                                          2004005092

Printed in the United States of America

The scanning, uploading and distribution of this book via the Internet or via any other
means without the permission of the publisher is illegal and punishable by law. Please
purchase only authorized electronic editions, and do not participate in or encourage electronic piracy of copyrighted materials. Your support of the author's rights is appreciated.

ONE

"DON'T FORGET, WE'RE ALL IN THIS TOGETHER."

Slouched in her seat at the back of the Oak Hills High auditorium, Keely Gilmore shifted her journal to glare up at the principal onstage. Every week during the Monday assembly Mrs. Hefti said the same thing in a slightly different way. Today's variation on her inspirational "We survived Strain 7" speech was heavy on unity. The creaky "We'll get through the hard times with each other's support and understanding" angle.

Keely wasn't convinced.

It had been almost two years since Strain 7 first struck. A swift, devastating monster, the respiratory virus managed to kill most people within a week of their first symptoms. Keely would never forget the surreal terror of the early days of the virus's spread in Los Angeles. The coughing and wheezing, the teachers dropping at school, people collapsing over the wheels of their cars. Strain 7 had moved through L.A. before anyone even knew its name. By the time the virus was recognized, Dad was gone and Keely's little sister, Bree, was sick. Sometimes Keely still dreamed about that horrible sound that Bree made in her final moments as she struggled to breathe, lungs filled with congestion. The death rattle, one reporter had called those sounds, back in the days when there was still real news coverage.

"The fact that you're here demonstrates a great deal of determination," the school principal prattled on, and Keely tapped her pen against her journal, then wrote: *Mrs. Hefti's optimism gives me a headache. As if any of these kids would be in school if they didn't have to be.*

Get caught cutting class and you went to jail—that was martial law for you. Ironic, how the very place that used to be Keely's refuge had become a prison. Ever since the reorganization of the country, students and teachers had been shifted and jostled so much that no one seemed to belong in school anymore. What was there to learn when a guy who used to direct B-level action movies now taught senior honors classes?

Keely started doodling a three-dimensional pyramid, thinking that the cryptic e-mails she'd received from Von were a whole lot more challenging than anything her new teachers had handed her. Von had started e-mailing her two weeks ago, with the very first mystery message.

The e-mail didn't say anything, it just had a quote from Marlowe, a passage Keely remembered learning when she'd studied iambic pentameter in her old honors English class.

> "Was this the face that launched a thousand ships,9
> And burnt the topless towers of Ilium?27
> Sweet Helen, make me immortal with a kiss.19
> Her lips suck forth my soul: see where it flies!"89

Keely knew that the passage referred to Helen of Troy, and in fact, she'd always thought that the idea of a face launching a bunch of ships was pretty melodramatic. But when she'd looked closely, she'd noticed the numbers at the end of each line.

What did they mean? She studied them for a pattern but found nothing.

Then suddenly she had seen it. So obvious— 9/27/1989. The numbers were about her—revealing that Von had personal information about her. September 27, 1989, was Keely's birthday.

At first she'd been freaked out. How had she managed to pick up a cyber-stalker? What did this "Von" person want from her? (Somehow she instantly assumed Von was male.) She guessed he'd gotten her e-mail address from a Web site. With libraries still closed, Keely had been all over the Web trying to download things to read. But if Von had her e-mail, what about her home address? Her phone number?

She hadn't responded, and she'd decided to tell her mom about the message.

But of course, that would have required her mother to be at home and awake long enough to hear something important from Keely, which didn't really happen much. Besides, the more Keely thought about it, she couldn't figure out why anyone out there would want to hurt her, and the e-mail hadn't been threatening in any clear way. In fact, it was the first interesting thing that had happened to her in a very long time. She finally wrote back, demanding to know who Von was and what was going on.

Von replied with an ancient Lucretius quote: "Nature ever by unseen bodies works." Keely realized that meant Von planned to remain a mystery. From the next few messages she deciphered that Von was "closer than you think" and that Von was not alone. And all this information had been encoded in Von's vast knowledge of classic poetry and literature. Soon Keely started to enjoy the challenge, and she wrote back with her own coded replies.

The puzzles had gone back and forth several times now, and Keely still didn't know what Von's name was. Well, from the e-mail address she assumed Von's last name was Moundum. But what kind of name was that? She had flipped through her mother's baby name book to find *Von,* which was also spelled *Vaughn, Vonn, Vonne.* . . .

Her pencil skidded off the page as a sputtering crackle from the vicinity of the ceiling was punctuated with a loud, sharp *pop* and the lights went out.

Someone near the front of the auditorium screamed. For a moment after that high-pitched shriek everyone seemed to freeze. Only one side of the cavernous room featured windows, which were set high in the wall, and the heavy maroon drapes were always closed now, supposedly to prevent the spread of viral spores.

As Keely held her breath, squinting into the inky darkness, her heart hammered with the memory of the day those other blackouts had happened more than a year ago, when the people who normally kept the world running were dying so fast and everything began to fall apart.

Obviously she wasn't the only one who remembered. A moment later the silence was replaced with the sound of panicked questions and seats creaking closed as students got up to shove into the aisles.

"Come on, move," urged the girl next to Keely. Her fingers brushed Keely's shoulder, and she withdrew her hand quickly.

"Don't panic," Mrs. Hefti shouted from the front of the auditorium. "I'm sure it's just a glitch with the generator. Please, don't run . . . and do not push!"

No one was listening.

Keely began to make out shapes in the shadows. The girl next to her hefted her backpack over her shoulder and moved closer, stepping on Keely's foot. "Come on, come on," she pressed.

"Give me a minute," Keely said. Her blood was still thrumming from the unexpected plunge into blackness, but it was just a regular power outage this time. It had to be. With so many buildings running on backup generators and reduced power, it was kind of amazing there hadn't been more blackouts. And there was nothing to fear from the dark except your own thoughts.

Which could be pretty frightening, of course.

Sliding her journal into her backpack, Keely stood up and edged into the crowd jamming the aisle. Down in front, Mrs. Hefti was still yelling instructions, which everyone was ignoring, including Mr. Marsters, one of the history teachers.

"Excuse me," he was saying, pushing into a knot of kids near the doors. His shiny bald head gleamed in the semidarkness. "I'm a little claustrophobic in these circumstances. I really have to get out, please. Come on. Let me through!"

Keely had heard he'd shaved his head after the virus because hair was a germ carrier. She'd also heard he used to be a production assistant at the local PBS station before Strain 7 hit and had taken the teaching position when it was clear nobody was going to be making documentaries again anytime soon. She couldn't believe she was expected to take U.S. Politics with him; he wasn't even a real teacher.

Beside her, Julie Mannino had strapped on a tie-dyed surgical mask. "It's just a little dark. No reason to maul each other." Julie's words were muffled by her mask. "Would you get off me, you freak!"

"Way to spread chaos, Mannino," shot back a tall boy who was sitting on the back of a chair in the first row. The slogan on his fluorescent T-shirt glowed neon green in the dark: Survivor: The World.

Julie ignored him and disappeared in the crowd swirling out into the hall.

Not far behind her, Keely was glad to peel away from the cluster of people and move toward the tile wall of the corridor. Here in the light kids craned their necks and checked around them, their panic giving way to amusement over having the school schedule disrupted.

Keely hung back and studied them. They were all strangers to her. Oh, she knew names and faces now, but after the reorganization only two kids from her old school had ended up here at Oak Hills, two kids she barely knew. Since busing used too much precious fuel and several schools had closed due to a shortage of teachers, students in L.A. had been redistricted to schools within walking distance. Knightsbridge, the private school Keely had attended since seventh grade, was way out in Pasadena.

And I'm supposed to get something out of this? Keely thought, eyeing the riotous crowd in the hallway. Half-baked teachers and displaced students. School had become a total waste of time. But then again, the government barely pretended that schools were intact to educate kids these days. High school was now a giant holding pen, a place to corral teens so Big Brother could keep watch more easily and effectively.

Sometimes, now that the Internet was back, she e-mailed friends from Knightsbridge, but only a few were left. Her best friends, Clio, Heather, and Zoe, were gone. Dead. Just like Eric. Just like her father and Bree.

It was no good thinking about that now. If she did, the grief would bloom into a fat lump in her throat, and then she'd be lost, standing here crying in front of everyone.

The students behind her were still pushing to get out of the auditorium, and she moved down the hall until her back was pressed against the cool tile. No one knew what to do. After assembly on Mondays they were usually excused in time for second-period class, but it was too early for that. Teachers here and there were shouting over the kids' voices, but only a few kids pretended to pay attention. Who could blame them? The lights were still out, and if they didn't come back on soon, the day would be a waste—no bells, no loudspeaker, just darkness and confusion.

Holding on to the necklace at her throat for the comfort of its sleek, familiar weight, Keely scanned the hallway and spotted Mrs. Ostrovsky, her English teacher, by the girls' bathroom. Across from her was a soldier standing straight and alert in front of the boys' bathroom, overseeing the mini-evacuation of the school. Keely wondered if he was happy to have a break in his usual routine of patrolling the hallway. There were soldiers or police officers (they had become basically the same thing) everywhere now, always lurking, waiting to grab anyone who broke the smallest rule or who even *seemed* about to break a rule. And when kids were hauled off by soldiers, you didn't usually see them again. All kinds of rumors flew around about what happened to them, and actually, it had been a while since any students had disappeared. No one was willing to risk acting up anymore when the punishment was obviously something a hell of a lot worse than detention.

Keely elbowed toward her teacher as an idea struck her. "Mrs. Ostrovsky?" she called.

Plastered to the wall, Mrs. O. clutched an armful of files. She looked like she was riding out the first symptoms of a migraine. "Yes, Keely?"

Go for it. Trying to look as sick as she could, Keely faked a long cough, letting the strain sting her throat. The hoarser, the better. "I feel awful."

Two girls beside Mrs. Ostrovsky shrank backward, tucking their chins to their shoulders. A boy in a decorated microfiber germ mask lunged away from her, stumbling into a senior girl who whirled on him angrily before he pointed at Keely.

"Have you been coughing long?" Mrs. Ostrovsky asked Keely. The teacher craned her neck backward so far, she looked like a scoliosis patient in a brace.

So paranoid. They all were. They'd survived the virus, but the thought of a germ—even the harmless, common-cold type—flipped them out.

Keely sniffled for effect and wiped her nose with the back of her hand. "Since yesterday," she mumbled, adding another weak cough for punctuation.

The teacher clutched her files to her chest as if they could protect her. "Go on home, then," she said. "I'll send a note to the office if we ever get out of this hallway, and I'll let the guard know you're permitted to leave."

Keely thanked her and backed away, sniffling loudly. The crowd parted before her like the Red Sea, and she had to bite the inside of her lip to keep from smiling.

It was a nasty thing to do; she knew it. With more than half of the global population wiped out by a virus, people were edgy. Illness of any kind sent them into attacks of paranoia. It freaked her out, too, when she stopped to think about it long enough. Experts like Mom said Strain 7 had run its course, but no one knew what dreaded spores might blow into town tomorrow. The next wave of the virus could be around the corner, a new strain or mutation breeding silently, collecting on the mouthpieces of phones and in the ventilation ducts of air-conditioning units, waiting to strike the grieving survivors of the first round.

But on days like this, Keely was beyond caring. What was the point in freaking out? Like it or not, she had another long, pointless day ahead of her. Nowhere to go, nothing to do.

Unlike two years ago, when there wasn't enough time in the day to do it all. Honors papers, SATs, movies and team projects with friends . . . Keely had been so happily crazed that she didn't realize how great things were, how lucky she was.

She kept her eyes on the floor as she moved down the hall toward the door. It wouldn't be smart to dance out the door, not when she was faking sick. The light from outside was brighter on the faded linoleum now—almost there.

"Keely! Hey, Keely! You okay?"

Startled, she looked up and saw Chris Cohen near the door. On the bulletin board behind him a makeshift poster someone had printed off the Internet warned, KISSING KILLS. KEEP YOUR DISTANCE—AND YOUR LIFE. In the background two teenagers sat at opposite ends of a sofa, smiling at each other, with the blue light of a TV screen flickering in the foreground.

"Keely," he called, "wait up."

Chris—just what she didn't need. She ignored him and kept walking, but Chris pushed through the crowd to reach her.

Once it would have made her life that a guy like him was so obviously into her—tall and lanky, with that athletic grace that made him look like he was gliding on air, when he was really just walking, like an ordinary human. Short, spiky brown hair and warm brown eyes—very cute. He was nice, too, not stuck up or arrogant at all.

But that just made it harder to say no to him. To make him understand that she wasn't interested in a new boyfriend or even a new friend. Not now, when she couldn't forget the people she had lost.

He caught up to her and elbowed her arm gently. "Where you headed in such a hurry?"

"Home," she said, her voice low. "I'm sick."

"Right." He rolled his eyes. "And I'm signing up to tour the Big Empty with the Strain Never band."

"Look, can I just get out of here before the assistant principal comes along and pushes me back toward the classrooms?"

He leaned in front of her and hit the bar to pop the door open. "Okay. If you're sick, I'll walk you home."

Keely stepped out into the milky October sunshine. "So you can go to jail for skipping school?"

"With all that chaos going on, I don't think they'll notice today." He stepped out and looked behind him suspiciously. "Besides, you don't really believe they have you drawn and quartered for something like cutting one afternoon, do you?"

"Who knows? Kids have been hauled off by soldiers at school in the past. And what about those two kids in New York?" Keely said, thinking back to the news stories on TV. "They were executed for stealing a truckload of batteries."

Chris winced. "Harsh. But I don't buy it. I mean, if you believe everything that's floating around, your head will explode."

Keely frowned up at him. "Oh, is that what happens?"

They fell silent as they reached the corner of Canyon and Los Alamos, once an intersection full of traffic, now eerily silent without the rushing of a million cars and trucks. A squat grey tank sat in the middle of the road, crushing the dried grass on the median strip.

"Do you think there's anyone inside?" Chris asked quietly.

"I wouldn't knock on the hatch and ask to borrow sugar," Keely said. "Don't look over there and maybe they'll leave us alone. Do you think the guys in that tank will believe I got permission to go home from Mrs. Ostrovsky?"

Chris picked up the pace. "Not a chance. Let's hope they're too busy eating protein bars to come out and play."

Once they'd cleared the tank, Keely relaxed and listened as Chris talked about his cousins from Minneapolis who were supposed to join the family here but had hit a few snags when they applied for travel papers. "So now they're stuck down in Mississippi."

"Scary," Keely said. "What's there?"

"Apparently not much for city kids."

"Well, thanks for the official escort," Keely said as she and Chris approached the flagstone walk in front of her house. Although Chris had seen the place before, she suddenly felt ashamed as the overgrown lawn came into view. The sidewalk was caked with a powder of tree pollen. The uneven, browning grass and the wild, sprouting bushes were a reminder that the world was out of control. Two years ago her father had prided himself on a lawn smooth enough to use as a putting green. Now there was no money for gardeners, no gas for lawn mowers and power tools, no manpower to handle the nonessential jobs like sculpting bushes and trimming grass.

Chris seemed to read her mind because he reached out and snapped off a wayward twig from one of the bushes. "You know, I could take care of this with a sharp pair of scissors. Got kitchen scissors?"

"It really doesn't matter," Keely said, turning away from him.

As she opened the front door, it occurred to her

that the inside of the house wasn't much better. Mom spent most of her time at the hospital research center, and Keely rarely felt the urge to play housekeeper. Abandoned shoes and jackets and books littered the living room, and the kitchen sink overflowed with dirty dishes. Keely glanced at the refrigerator door, where she fastened notes to her mother, somehow still imagining that Dr. Gilmore might take a moment to read one. A bunch of notes were stuck behind a magnet, unread, and the weight of the paper had caused the magnet to slide halfway down the stainless steel door.

Chris headed for the fridge. "Got anything good?"

"If it isn't green and fuzzy, it's yours," Keely said as she wandered into the den and flopped onto the couch. Now that she was free, she wondered how to spend the afternoon. She'd read just about every book she could get her hands on, but she was expecting an e-mail from the elusive Von.

"Your fridge light is on," Chris called from the kitchen. "You got power here."

She pressed the power button on the remote and the television screen flickered on. "Looks like the blackout was just at school."

Chris appeared with a clear-wrapped Twinkie. "How the hell did you score these?"

Keely shrugged. "I told you, my mother is an important person."

"Dr. Gilmore . . ." He held the Twinkie as if it were a microphone. "On the virus front, battling new and dangerous diseases."

"That's what they say," Keely said, letting her head sink into the couch. But the truth was, she had lost faith in Mom a long time ago. What good was an immunologist when a virus raged through the population unchecked?

Chris bit into the Twinkie, watching the TV screen. "Do you think they'll have anything on the school blackout?"

"Let's see." Keely turned up the volume on the news show. The GBN news anchor was intoning the usual reminders about lights curfew and restricted water use. The Government Broadcasting Network was one of the only channels on the air now, aside from the WB, which showed mostly old reruns of sitcoms and sci-fi dramas. If she had to sit through one more episode of *Buffy the Vampire Slayer,* she'd scream. Once the idea of a small, blond female superhero had been fascinating, but now the show only served as a reminder that no one had been able to save the world from Strain 7.

Keely dropped the remote on a cushion. "Nope. Oak Hills High is just not hot news. That school is lame, anyway."

"At least your school and your whole town didn't get shut down. You got to stay in your house," Chris said. It was a sore spot with him, having to leave his family's home in Nevada and move west to California. Not that she blamed him. Still, he wasn't the only displaced student.

"It's not my school," Keely replied. "But I'm sorry

you had to move. Maybe someday you and your dad can go back?"

"Not in this lifetime," he said, turning up the volume as a map of the United States flashed on the screen.

"In an exclusive GBN interview this morning, President George MacCauley announced that the reorganization of the Central States is nearly final," said the newscaster. "The plan was initiated more than a year ago when it became clear that the surviving U.S. workforce was unable to maintain the infrastructure throughout the country. The president stated that the evacuation of the central United States was vital to maintaining the nation's infrastructure, and he thanked the citizens for their cooperation in making the move swiftly and efficiently."

"Right," Chris said. "Like we had a choice."

Keely stared at the map. Vast areas of land were marked in red as "Evacuated Zones." The states of Nevada, Colorado, Idaho, Montana, Illinois, Michigan, Ohio, Missouri . . . just to name a few. It was a frightening geography lesson. President MacCauley had ordered that everyone in the middle of the country move south, east, or west, and the people who'd survived Strain 7 in the heartland of the country had had no choice but to comply. Just as they hadn't had a choice in making George MacCauley president in the first place.

Formerly the anchor of a political news show in Washington, D.C., MacCauley had somehow ended up spearheading the effort to set up a new government to replace the one that had been decimated by the virus.

He'd rallied support behind him with his apparent calm and control in the midst of all the confusion, and no one had objected when he basically assumed the office—especially once his army was in place, marching through the streets. The whole "governed by the people, for the people" democracy thing lost a lot of steam when people were dying all around you. Instead of senators, representatives, and all the rest of the old government system, it had become just President MacCauley and his board, a group of yes-men and -women who carried out MacCauley's rules.

Soon enough martial law was the norm, and nobody seemed to care that there was still a curfew after all these months or that the word *election* hadn't been mentioned by anyone in power.

"It's scary to think most of this country is abandoned," Keely said. "The Big Empty," she murmured, using the nickname people had given the evacuated area.

"I'm not sure it's so empty," Chris said. "Sometimes I imagine there's a family living in my old house. Some kid living my old life, getting his driver's permit, trying out for the tennis team."

Keely shook her head as the television showed busloads of people rolling down a desert highway. Close-ups of immigrant faces from Oklahoma and Wisconsin, some waving, some just staring. A bizarre American tale. "Reno is a ghost town now," Keely said quietly. "All those cities are."

"Haven't you heard about the renegades out there?

Bands of people who defied MacCauley's orders. Outlaws in the Big Empty, living large on what's left in the cities and towns."

"Maybe." Keely shrugged. She'd heard the rumors, but her new attitude was skepticism. Informed skepticism. "Maybe not."

As pictures flashed on the TV screen, Keely felt a surprising sense of sadness at the abandoned homes and dreams. Strain 7 had killed more people than she could fathom, but it hadn't stopped there. The virus had destroyed the lives and dreams of survivors too.

And hope. Worst of all, it had destroyed hope.

TWO

SLINGING HIS RIFLE OVER HIS SHOULDER, DIEGO SANDOVAL stepped beneath the cover of a black oak, cursing under his breath. He'd spent his entire life in this stretch of Missouri, capturing lightning bugs in the woods in summer, tramping to school through the December snow. Some nights when he lay bored in the hammock waiting for shooting stars, he'd sworn he knew every inch of his grandmother's property. But right now, unless he dug up every inch, he was out of luck.

His grandmother had been a hoarder—usually a good thing. But when it came to hiding her treasure, she'd succeeded a little too well. The rough map she'd sketched was like a kindergartner's drawing. The *X* scratched under something marked *Big Black Oak* wasn't much help to Diego in a forest filled with tall black oaks.

He was looking for a box of batteries, candles, cornmeal, rice, and Nonnie's home-canned pickles. Since his grandmother died two months ago, he'd been living off the supplies they'd kept hidden behind the toolshed, but those were wearing thin. Besides, Diego was so sick of canned peaches, he could puke just thinking about the sugary syrup. If he didn't find Nonnie's rations, he was in for some long, dark, hungry nights. Soon.

The sudden crack of a twig made him whirl around.

Twenty feet away a doe stared at him, frozen in place. He watched her, fascinated. The animal was healthy, after a long summer free to roam every field and clearing for miles, grazing her fill. Hell, she was probably the one who'd been nibbling at the corn he and his grandmother had planted.

The rifle hung from his shoulder, a cold deadweight. He couldn't shoot her. She looked just like Bambi's mother, for one, and by the time he swung the rifle into firing position, she'd be long gone anyway.

Plus—small detail here—he wasn't big on the idea of skinning a deer. A rabbit he could handle—and had, plenty of times in the last six months. He hated every minute of the slaughter, but you do a lot of things you hate to survive. Rabbits had kept him from going hungry, but a deer was so big. . . .

Which would mean lots of hot, filling meals. A stab of hunger went through him. Venison was delicious if you cooked it right and not terrible if you overcooked

it, either. This was survival, not some Disney movie—
and Bambi was nowhere in sight.

Bambi. What a dumb name for a buck anyway.

He started to slide his arm up slowly, just an inch, to
get his fingers around the barrel of the gun, but the doe
wasn't stupid. She bounded off into the forest's shade, a
flash of sleek brown, her white tail winking at him as
she disappeared into the trees.

"Real stealthy," he muttered, letting his arm drop to
his side. Back to the search for pickles.

The batteries and cornmeal were more important,
but he was down to the bottom of the rice too, so that
was only a once-a-week treat now. Hard to believe that
he used to gripe when Mom bought the wrong brand of
frozen waffles.

Spotting another tall black oak, he went to the base
of the trunk and poked around in the leaves with the
barrel of the rifle. He should have checked Nonnie's
maps months ago, but he'd never thought he'd be digging this stuff up alone. They'd split up to bury things
once or twice, an idea he'd considered pretty efficient
at the time, since that was at the height of the military's
patrols through the area, looking for holdouts who
refused to leave and confiscating any supplies, edible or
not. Nonnie's house had been tossed twice, but he and
Nonnie had already buried most of the important stuff
around their property, and the soldiers had been fool
enough to leave the propane tanks that heated the
house and water.

"Just call me a renegade," Nonnie had whispered

the first time they'd had to hide. She'd grinned at him from inside the trunk of a huge cedar they'd found in a deadfall. Clearing out the worst of the bugs and debris, they'd rolled it over so she could crawl inside it while Diego lay hidden beneath a makeshift blanket of evergreen branches beside her.

She'd been a tough old broad. His heart squeezed painfully as he pictured the grin she'd flashed at him, her leathery cheeks dirty and scratched. Nobody, not even the U.S. Army, was going to tell her the state of Missouri was being evacuated. "Honey, if I made it through Strain 7, there's no soldier or general who's going to take me in now," she'd told him repeatedly. At the time it seemed like Nonnie could survive anything. It sort of added to Diego's shock when he found her cold in bed one morning. Died in her sleep. He figured it was her heart, but that was just a guess.

Without her, life in the Big Empty was almost too tough to bear. Being so alone that you could hear your own heartbeat at night. Diego hated it, but he didn't see any choice. He'd seen pictures of the cities east and west, New York with its abandoned skyscrapers—no one was wasting electricity on elevators anymore—and Los Angeles with tanks parked on the corners. Right now life outside the Big Empty seemed to suck even more than life in it.

But it was boring here, and lonely. Sometimes Diego fantasized that he was the last person on earth. Two weeks ago he'd been so bored, he'd hauled Mom's china out to the nearest pasture and engaged in a little target practice. If he was going to be the last man on earth, might as well go out with a bang.

He checked his watch, then looked up into the canopy of leaves to gauge the sun's position. Turning west, he kicked at twigs and damp mulch as he walked. Time for plan B. He headed toward the dry creek bed where he'd buried a small carton of Bisquick, a bag of sugar, and some fruit roll-ups—each packed in a plastic Ziploc, double-wrapped in garbage bags.

"Oh, well," he said aloud. If he couldn't have pickles by candlelight, he could have pancakes for breakfast.

He stepped into a clearing just beyond a tight knot of oaks and tipped his face up to catch the last of the afternoon sun. *Yeah,* he thought, shielding his eyes against the sun. *Pancakes would be good.* His ears were tuned to the ring of some late-summer cicadas when he heard the voice.

"Hands up! Stop right there."

Holy crap.

Diego froze, his heart hammering against his ribs. Who the hell was that? Slowly he turned to look over his shoulder.

Oh, man. Bad news. A soldier, pointing a rifle right at him.

Diego swallowed hard, fear bitter and metallic in his mouth. It was all over now. A soldier on patrol would take him away and stick him in some group home in a distant city, and he would never see his farm again.

The farm his parents and grandparents—and his grandmother's parents before them—had built from scratch. The farm where he'd promised Nonnie he'd stay until the panic about the virus was over and "those knuckleheads in the government come to their senses," as she'd put it.

He adjusted one foot to pivot toward the soldier, but that freaked the guy out. "Put down your weapon!" the soldier shouted. "Now, boy!"

His weapon . . . ? Crap, the rifle.

"This . . ." Diego realized how it must look. "It's just for hunting."

"Put it down, boy!" the soldier growled.

Boy? What the hell? The soldier didn't look much more than twenty himself.

Anger flooded through Diego. He wasn't hurting anybody—he couldn't even shoot a damn deer. What right did this guy have to order him around? To invade Nonnie's land and drag Diego off?

"I said put it down," the soldier called roughly. His weapon was jammed against his shoulder in firing position. "And I mean it."

Diego stood his ground, staring. This was still America, right? Soldiers couldn't just shoot people for no reason.

Then he heard a sharp, unmistakable *click* as the soldier cocked the gun.

Diego swallowed.

"I want that weapon on the ground," the soldier shouted, taking two steps toward Diego. "You're on restricted land here."

You're on my *land,* Diego wanted to shout, but he kept his mouth shut.

"For the last time, I'm telling you to put that weapon down," the soldier barked, but his voice was unsteady.

Diego didn't think about his next move; he just turned and ran.

"Stop!" the soldier shouted.

His senses heightened by adrenaline, Diego felt sweat beading on his upper lip. He could smell the rotting mulch of the forest bed, hear the cry of a distant bird . . .

And the crunch of dry leaves as the soldier followed him.

Crap. Nonnie would be pissed if he got shot after all they'd been through.

After a minute his lungs burned in his chest and his legs began to protest, but he didn't stop. He ran full out, the way he had as a kid when the school bell rang.

He ran for his life.

THREE

As Michael Bishop came out of the subway at West 4th Street and made his way toward the small Greenwich Village apartment he shared with his father, he realized that he would never make it back to the apartment before curfew tonight. Once the curfew hit Manhattan, the city just about rolled up its sidewalks, but he didn't intend to stay with Maggie after what he had to say to her. Michael had been dragging his feet on this breakup for weeks, caught in a mixture of guilt, obligation, and lust.

As he noticed his buddies Kenny and Jeff manning Father Demo Square in their military fatigues, he wished he could stick around to play a few rounds of cards. Michael had befriended the local crew of soldiers after he and his father moved down here from the Upper West Side, after the electricity shortage had made it too costly to run elevators up to the thirtieth-floor penthouse that Michael and his parents had once called home.

Now, after the relocation, Michael and his dad were lucky to have scored a third-story walk-up in the Village. "It's like a return to the Gilded Age," his father had said, trying to make the most of it. "Did you know that around the turn of the century Fourteenth Street was the hub of the city? People considered it a trip to the country to venture above Fiftieth." Typical Dad, clinging to old Manhattan's charms.

"Hey, it's the Bishop!" Kenny straightened from his perch on the square's park bench and touched his fingertips to his chin.

Michael returned the gesture—a form of greeting that had surfaced when the spread of Strain 7 made handshakes dangerous. "Guys, what's up?"

"Just another pleasantly boring afternoon on the Isle of York," Jeff said, tipping back his helmet. "The president says the relocation is a success and life is good."

"It'd be better if girls started wearing short skirts again," Kenny said as he eyed two girls in flowing ankle-length skirts heading toward Sixth Avenue.

"Prairie-wear," Jeff muttered. "You know, I grew up in Kansas and our girls didn't wear skirts like that."

"It's reaction fashion," Michael said, watching as the girls passed a middle-aged, greying man lost in thought.

It was Michael's father, his briefcase tucked under

the sleeve of his elegant jacket, a fall suit from two years ago—before the virus. Dad must have finished with his meeting downtown. Michael waved, but Dad didn't seem to see him.

Graham Bishop didn't notice much these days. He refused to acknowledge the unpleasant realities of life in New York. He simply didn't see the soldiers in the streets or the fires burning above Columbus Circle or the hungry people lined up for food outside the school auditoriums. A brief glimpse of high-voltage reality would shoot Dad's entire disposition to hell. No more of that "Think positive!" and "Sunny-side up!"

Although his father drove Michael crazy, making him jump through hoops in the office and pay service calls on alarms that should have been dismantled months ago, Michael did have compassion for him. He was lonely with Michael's mom gone, and underneath that cheery facade, Michael realized he was scared.

Everyone was scared. People dealt with it in different ways. Michael befriended soldiers and people who could get their hands on coffee beans and the guys who drove the subway trains. He was determined to make allies in this new world.

Graham Bishop used his energy to deny that there was a new world.

"Hey, where's that pretty girlfriend of yours?" Kenny asked Michael. "I haven't seen her around for a while."

"Yeah, and you probably won't," Michael said. "Which is why I might be late getting home tonight. Got some things to take care of. Think you can slip me in under the bar?" It never hurt to clear the way. With martial law in place, penalties for the tiniest offense could be severe.

"No problem," Kenny said. "We're here all night."

"What's the matter, Bishop?" Jeff asked. "Maggie dump you?"

Michael took in a deep breath. "I wish." He'd been putting off the big breakup until he felt Maggie was on solid ground, getting used to being on her own.

"What?" Jeff adjusted his gun belt. "Don't tell me you've got another girl."

"Nothing like that." Michael didn't want to get into the complicated reasons for breaking up with someone you've outgrown. "I'm just trying to streamline my life. More work, less play."

That made both soldiers laugh. "Yeah, right," Kenny said sarcastically.

"Seriously. Dad is bringing in a government contract. They're talking about letting us wire half of D.C. with our top-of-the-line alarm system."

"That's impressive," Kenny said. "Would you put in a good word for us when you're wiring the Oval Office?"

"No problem," Michael said as he headed across the square to the apartment. The sooner he got changed out of his work clothes and back on the train, the sooner he'd be finished with this whole awkward episode in his life.

I won't miss hanging out up here, Michael thought as he passed a boarded-up pizza place on West 49th Street where he and Maggie used to grab slices and sodas after school. Now the rich aroma of pizza baking had given way to the burnt smell that wafted down from uptown, where the fire department let fires rage unchecked. Michael had seen it happen to the towering glass apartment building that used to face their penthouse. That was when he knew the mayor's orders had to be heeded: move downtown if you want any form of city services.

His feet followed the familiar path west, to the eighth-floor apartment Maggie had taken in the reorganization. For a long time after the virus had passed, it was nice to be up there with Maggie after the curfew, to feel her, warm and soft beside him, in the flickering candlelight or the dim glow of a camp lantern. Maggie had a gift, a way of shutting out the world and making him believe it was just the two of them. And Maggie's grandfather had never seemed to mind when he stayed over, although sometimes it was hard to tell if he'd even noticed in the first place. Even before the virus the old guy wasn't completely there, always drifting in and out, occasionally talking to ghosts of his past.

Sometimes Michael wondered if Maggie was all there herself. She just didn't seem to be able to get that life was different now. Michael was sick of telling her that it pissed him off when she cut school or when she skipped the lines at the free kitchens and used up her grandfather's valuable cash and coupons at the local deli. She always just laughed it off, even when he blew up at her after she burned up batteries in three flashlights for a disco ball effect. He began to wonder if they had anything in common anymore, anything to keep them together, other than the fact that they had been together before the virus.

Then Grandpa Logan had died of a stroke a few months ago, and Michael felt an increasing sense of dread about what that meant for him and Maggie. He was all she had. It gave him an overwhelming sense of responsibility—one he had never really signed on for. And Maggie had grown even more reckless, more difficult for Michael to be around without getting frustrated or angry. He didn't want to play her games, or pretend everything was still the same, or take risks. He wanted to navigate this new world successfully, to thrive. It was time to move on, to figure things out and get his future together.

So this was it—he'd finally decided he was going to do it, make a clean break. They'd had something together once, a long time ago, but it was already way past the expiration date.

Michael was so focused on his breakup speech that he almost didn't notice Maggie up ahead. Tucked into a group of her local friends—losers as far as Michael was concerned—she giggled as one of the guys jammed something into his jacket and followed her into Henry's Deli.

"Maggie!" Michael called from the street, but she was already inside. He cut over to the deli, skirting around a man in a sandwich board with the scrawled message: *The end already came! Did you miss it?!*

Just as he reached the deli, its door crashed open

and Maggie's three friends burst out, their arms full of groceries. Where was Maggie?

"Tony!" Michael called to one of them.

The kid glanced back nervously, then took off running after the other two.

What the hell was going on? Through the window Michael didn't see anyone in the shop, though the place was a mess. Dented cans of cat food and baby formula lay sideways on the shelves, and a box of candles had spilled out onto the dirty linoleum, along with a few packages of AA batteries. The shop had been trashed.

He pushed into the deli and immediately saw the cash register gaping open, empty. A few yellow government-issue coupons had drifted to the floor, but it was clear the place had been robbed.

Maggie's loser friends had robbed the deli.

"Oh, man," Michael whispered aloud. This was not good.

"You!"

Michael swung around to see Henry, the owner, stumbling toward him, a hand pressed to the back of his head. Someone must have clocked him.

"You . . ." Henry seethed, closing in on Michael. "And her!" The deli owner pointed as Maggie emerged from a door behind him—the bathroom.

Michael held his hands up to Henry as the scenario became clear. Those stupid kids had set her up. Get Maggie to ask for the bathroom, then take down Henry and empty the register.

"Henry?" Maggie seemed genuinely surprised. Michael

didn't think it was an act, but Henry wasn't buying it.

Henry grabbed Maggie's arm, then wheeled around to glare at Michael. "The two of you! You're not getting away with this."

"She didn't know," Michael said, jumping to Maggie's defense. "And I just walked in on this. I wasn't with them!" Michael pointed toward the door.

Henry's face closed as he crossed his arms. "You were all in this together."

The bell over the door jingled, and another man walked in. "I saw them, Henry," he said, his cheeks flushed. "I called the police. These kids are going to pay, big time."

"But we didn't . . . I mean, I didn't—" Michael stammered, feeling the blood drain from his face. Big time, like those kids who'd stolen the batteries? Big time, like with their lives?

"Oh, right, just a coincidence, huh?" Henry twisted Maggie's arm and shoved her toward the counter. When he turned around, Michael saw that blood from his head had dripped down the back of his shirt.

At the sight, Michael felt the shop closing in around him. If Maggie was found guilty of robbery and assault, the penalty would be severe. Death.

Michael blinked.

And Henry thinks I was in on it.

The deli owner let go of Maggie's arm to reach for a stack of paper towels. Michael glared at Maggie, then cut his gaze toward the door. *"Run,"* he mouthed. *"Go!"*

She stared at him blankly for half a second. Then

she flew, a blur of dirty blond hair and a tan peacoat.

Michael sprinted after her. The stranger jerked up in surprise and made a last-minute grab for him, but Michael lunged away and burst through the open door.

"Run!" he hissed at Maggie, who had slowed down to glance back at him. There was no time to stop.

"Where?" Maggie gasped. "The subway? I can't go very fast in these shoes."

"Just come on!" Michael yelled. He sprinted ahead of her, then stopped and threw up his hands. What would it take to light a fire under her? "Take the damn shoes off!"

As Maggie fumbled with her shoes, Michael's mind clicked ahead. What next? Where was the best place to go?

He thought of safe places. His apartment. The office. The library. The guard station at Father Demo Square.

No. None of those places would be safe anymore. Kenny and Jeff wouldn't even be able to speak to him, let alone offer protection. And his father—it would kill Graham Bishop to learn that his son was accused of a crime that could cost him his life.

Despite Michael's innocence, his life was ruined. Over.

"I can't do this," Maggie gasped behind him. "This is killing my feet."

Michael was tempted to let her sit on the curb while he ducked into a hiding place for a few weeks. For once, Maggie could deal with her mess without him.

But somehow he couldn't walk away. He couldn't let her die for acting like an idiot. He couldn't leave her on the curb, pathetic and helpless. Not with those police sirens screaming down Columbus Avenue.

"The C train," Michael said. In the strobe of the lights flashing red and blue in the twilight, he grabbed Maggie's elbow and tugged her down the subway steps.

FOUR

WHILE CHRIS ROOTED THROUGH THE KITCHEN, KEELY CHECKED her e-mail. The little white envelope that indicated incoming messages appeared. There was one from Kevin Carlton, Eric's friend; she'd read that later, when she was alone. And wait . . . *Yes.* There was one from Von. Her pulse sped up at the sight of the familiar address in her in-box. She quickly clicked on the white envelope and scanned the short message:

To: Keely Gilmore
From: Von Moundum
If you're looking for an afternoon activity after a break-fast of scrambled eggs, try Aldous Huxley in Latin.

She picked up a pencil and tapped it against the open calendar. Scrambled eggs—was Von trying to tell her that something in the messages was a word scramble? An anagram? Hmm.

Then there was that Aldous Huxley comment. Keely knew he was the author of a science-fiction book, but she couldn't remember the title. She went to her room and rooted through her old English literature textbooks, and eventually found a list of titles. Huxley's most famous book was *Brave New World*. "He wants me to read *Brave New World* in Latin?" she muttered. That couldn't be right.

Unless Von meant she should translate the title itself into Latin. Which, fortunately, she could do. Keely had spent two years studying Latin at Knightsbridge. What was the word for *new*?

Novo.

Her heart beat faster as she looked back at the letters on her computer screen.

VON MOUNDUM

She crossed out the letters *V* and *N*, and both *Os*, suddenly knowing what she would come up with.

The letters that were left spelled *mundum*. World.

Novo mundum. An anagram for Von Moundum. And loosely translated, it could mean *new world*.

Keely sat back. New world—what did that mean? There'd been rumors about rebels out there, as Chris had mentioned. But what if there was actually a whole organized group of people, forming a *new world*?

"What's wrong?" Chris asked.

"Nothing," she said quickly. She was trying not to get too excited. Not long ago she'd dreamed of being recruited by Ivy League colleges, but now that didn't even mean a thing. But this—this could be a chance. A chance to have something resembling a life again.

I've always been intrigued by Brave New World. *I'd like to read more,* Keely typed.

She clicked on send before she lost her nerve.

"What's that, homework?" Chris asked, nodding at her doodles.

She clicked the message closed quickly. "Just goofing around. E-mail is one of the last uncensored pleasures."

"You think so?" He cocked his head. "Are you trying to tell me I'm losing my touch?"

"You never had it," she teased him, but immediately bit her lip. There'd never been chemistry between them— at least, not on her end. She reached for her charm necklace, fiddling nervously.

"Ouch." He put the plate down and leaned against the back of the couch. "You're rubbing that necklace like it's going to make me go away in a cloud of smoke."

Keely's fist closed around the white-gold sunburst pendant. In the months since Bree had died, it had become a kind of talisman, Keely's only tangible connection to her sister. Keely had given Bree the charm and chain for her thirteenth birthday.

"This necklace belonged to my sister," Keely said. "And this watch was my dad's." She held out her wrist to show him the fat silver Rolex her dad had worn.

"That's nice," Chris said softly. "Keeping them close like that." He reached out and touched her, his hand warm on her shoulder.

It was too much.

All she could think about was the way she'd felt when Eric had touched her—that electric tingle that had lit her up inside. That wasn't something she could allow herself to feel—not with Chris, not with anyone. She jerked away from him, letting his hand drop abruptly.

Chris's mouth set in a grim line. "I didn't mean it like that." His eyes narrowed. "I just want to be your friend, Keely."

She swallowed hard, her throat tight. "I had friends, Chris. Didn't you? Good friends, people I'd known forever. People I loved. They're gone, and they're never coming back. I know that, I'm not stupid—but it doesn't mean I'm ready to replace them. It's not like changing a battery, you know."

"Don't you think I know that?" His voice hardened. "I lost friends too. But I'm still alive, Keely. *We're* still alive. Still walking around, living and breathing. And those people we lost wouldn't want us to live in gloom because they're gone."

"I don't live in gloom," she snapped. "But you can't force me to be happy, Chris. Okay?"

He paused, holding her gaze, staring at her with an intensity that gave her a familiar weak sensation in her stomach, the crumbling that meant she might cry any second. Then finally he just nodded. "Okay."

Without another word he grabbed his backpack from

the sofa and headed toward the door. A moment later she winced as the front door banged shut, its small glass window rattling.

Turning back to the computer screen, she nearly gasped. There was a new message from Von. From Novo Mundum:

> If you liked that book, you should try these:
> *The History of Griffith*, by Parker Quatre
> *Today's Child*, by Ineo Carousel

Keely stared at the e-mail. She'd never heard of those books or the authors. It was a code for her, she was sure. She ran her pencil under the first title. *Griffith,* by Parker Quatre.

Did they mean Griffith Park? And *quatre* was French for the number four. Griffith Park at four?

Yes, four o'clock today—*Today's Child*. She didn't understand the meaning of "Ineo," and the dictionary didn't help, but she knew there was an old carousel in Griffith Park. Was that the meeting place? The carousel in Griffith Park at four today?

She e-mailed back: *Will definitely check out your recommendations.*

Yes, she'd meet "Von" in Griffith Park. She knew she should be at least a little nervous, but for some reason she wasn't. She trusted this mystery person—and she couldn't wait to find out what Von had to offer.

FIVE

MOVE YOUR BUTTS, PEOPLE!

Amber Polnieki elbowed past a man holding a kid by the hand in the crowded waiting room of the Orlando bus station. She ignored his offended "Hey!" as she ran for the ladies' room. So she was rude. It would be ruder to puke all over the kid's Mickey Mouse backpack, wouldn't it?

And if the gigantic woman in front of her didn't get the hell out of the way, *she* was going to get a nasty surprise all over the back of that circus tent of a dress.

"Excuse me," Amber muttered, angling between the female Hulk and her pile of luggage lumped directly in the path to the ladies' room. "In a hurry here."

"Yeah, well, we all are, honey," the woman snapped, her third chin jiggling.

Amber wanted to ask the woman how she sustained those chins on government-issue protein bars, but just then her stomach heaved. No time to stop for an argument.

She leaped over the battered suitcases, rounded the corner into the foul-smelling restroom, and stumbled into an empty stall just in time to retch up most of her breakfast.

Sweating and panting, she shuddered as the last wave of nausea rolled through her. Damn. She reached back and slammed the stall door shut as an afterthought. Like she needed anyone else to witness her humiliation. Although come to think of it, screw them. They weren't the ones barfing their guts up, were they?

She was a living snow globe, she thought. Every morning—and sometimes afternoons, too—someone shook up her insides and she spewed. Just not sparkly white snow, unfortunately.

Struggling out of her bowl-hugging crouch to flush the toilet, she perched on the edge of the seat, swung her backpack into her lap, and dug inside for a hard candy. Saltines were supposed to be better, but try finding those anymore, even stale ones.

She unwrapped the butterscotch and popped it into her mouth, then gagged. Not a good idea.

She made her way to a sink, spitting the candy into the overflowing trash bin first. The cool water felt good on her cheeks, and she cupped her hands to rinse out her mouth, too. Better.

Well, at least she *felt* better. One look in the mirror over the row of sinks made her want to gag again. Her white-blond hair straggled out of its ponytail, and her blue eyes were bloodshot and puffy.

She dropped her backpack on the floor and pawed through it for a hairbrush. Everything she owned was stuffed into the ancient nylon bag, and it didn't add up to much. Then there was the big problem of what she *didn't* have, like the traveling authorization to get on the bus to New Orleans. A bus she needed to board in thirty minutes.

Who'd have thought getting around would be such a major pain? You needed freaking papers to get on a bus—even after you'd paid. The whole country was being treated like a bunch of bad kids who needed a hall pass. Amber had hated hall passes when she'd even bothered with school. And she'd never been the follow-the-rules type in the first place.

Hairbrush in hand, she worked the elastic band out of her ponytail and attacked her snarled hair. A white-haired grandmotherly type walked up to the next sink and gave Amber one of those "My, aren't you sweet?" smiles she hated.

The world looked at her and saw a skinny, angel-faced twelve-year-old, and it always tempted Amber to let loose a string of curses. She was fifteen, not some little kid.

"All alone, dear?" the woman asked, rinsing her hands under the sputtering spray.

Oh, no, my pimp is waiting for me outside, she
wanted to snap. But she just smiled as she skinned her
hair back and fastened the elastic. "Yes, ma'am," she
said, adding a little syrup to her voice. "But I'm fine."

"Brave girl." The woman shook her head and
nudged the air dryer with her elbow before sticking her
hands under the heat. "So many children—well, so
many people—are alone now. I never thought I'd outlive my children, and it hardly seems fair, if you know
what I mean. It just doesn't make sense that I would
live on instead of them. A mother should never have to
outlive her children."

"It's tough," Amber said, wishing the woman would
just shut up.

"I'm sorry, dear. You're young, at least, with your
whole life ahead of you. And even now . . . Granted, the
world has changed, but life must be worth something."

Is it? Amber wondered bleakly. Then two teenage
girls walked in, breaking the moment. Amber pretended
to dig in her backpack until the old woman picked up her
wheeled suitcase and left, the air dryer still blowing.

"He can't deal, you know?" one girl said to the other
as they walked up to the mirror. She was tall and thin,
but the parts that counted—the ones she was showing
off in her tight sweater and long straight skirt—would
have been right at home on a Barbie doll. She ran a
hand through her thick, honey-blond hair, studying her
reflection. "So after this weekend in New Orleans—my
last fling—it's off to this total convent of a school he
heard about. I swear to God, it's like Paranoia Central

at my house. I caught him spraying antibacterial stuff on the computer keyboard the other day. Next thing you know, he's going to have me shopping at Aluminum Is Us for a tinfoil hat."

Her friend—shorter and way less glossy—chimed in with, "Yeah, but boarding school can be fun, right? No parents, no—"

"No nothing," the blonde cut in, rolling her eyes. "There's nothing fun about anything anymore. I swear, I'd give my CD collection for a cheeseburger and fries."

She looked like the type who'd puke it up minutes later on purpose, Amber thought, but she didn't blame her for the craving. One more "chocolate-cheesecake-flavored" protein shake and she was going to start eating her own hair.

Amber found the stub of a black eyeliner in the bottom of her pack and leaned close to the mirror to outline her eyes, determined to listen as long as she could. Miss Thing obviously had bucks, or at least her daddy did, and she clearly had travel papers as well—to New Orleans, no less.

Could be a score.

"It's so cool that you asked me to come this weekend, Faith," the dark-haired girl said. "Especially with Jackson there and all."

"Thinking of making the big move, Dee?" Faith smirked into the mirror, waving a tube of lip gloss at her friend. "Did you bring along something hot to wear?"

"Well, I don't know about that." Dee blushed. "I'm

happy just looking at him, you know? Actual touching is, like, Advanced Seduction, and I'm still on Flirting for Dummies."

"Come on, what does it matter now anyway? Hey, watch this for me, okay?" Faith dropped her backpack at her friend's feet, then popped into a stall. "Besides, I can tell you exactly what he likes."

Ooooh. That hurt. Amber cut her eyes sideways just in time to catch the outrage on Dee's face. Dee spun toward the mirror, then paced toward the exit, then spun again, pressing her hands to her cheeks. Quietly she ducked into a far stall and shut the door.

Poor little lamb, Amber thought, eyeing the abandoned backpack.

Just as Faith called through the stall door, "God, this place is nasty. I swear, it smells like someone puked in here," Amber was hoisting her own backpack over her shoulder and neatly scooping up Faith's with her free hand.

She walked out of the bathroom without looking back and glanced around for a security guard. Pasting a scared expression on her face, she ran up to him.

"Sir, I was just in the ladies' room over there"—she pointed with a trembling finger—"and there's a bag on the floor. This girl—blond, kind of tall and pretty—she walked out and left it behind, but she was acting funny while she was in there, and I think the bag might be, you know . . . ticking."

The security guard stiffened and fumbled for his radio.

"Code seven, east end ladies' room. I repeat, code seven. . . ."

Amber took a tentative step backward as the guard hurried off. In another two minutes the restroom would be surrounded by soldiers with automatic rifles. That should keep Faith busy for a little while.

She melted into the crowd, then cut toward the gate for New Orleans—gate nine. The bus was already parked in the slip, not taking passengers yet. Amber perched on the empty end of a bench and flipped open the stolen backpack. Better make sure the travel papers were all set.

The ticket was right on top—one way to New Orleans, along with travel papers and a big, fat wad of food-and-essentials coupons. Way to go, Faith!

Amber dug a little deeper. Her hand closed around the smooth, slender edge of a laptop. Could it be? It had killed Amber to leave her own laptop behind, but without access to a phone and power source, it was sort of useless. Biting her lower lip, she took it out for a quick exam. This baby had a wireless connection, plus an extra battery pack. Major score.

She tucked the laptop away along with the tickets, then flipped open Faith's ID.

Faith Stank.

Ha—that was something. Too bad she'd lifted the ID of someone with a name like that. No chance of just slipping by under the radar. Especially when there was that political guy, one of the members of President MacCauley's board, with the same name, Melvin Stank—nicknamed Smelly Stank, of course, by Amber and her friends.

Wait a second, was Faith Melvin Stank's daughter? That would certainly explain the store of coupons and the sleek laptop.

So now I'm a board member's daughter, Amber thought as she leaned over the two backpacks to rearrange things, putting her belongings into Faith's pack so she'd only have to carry one around. *How far can I get before the police catch on?*

She grinned.

No time like the present to find out.

SIX

DIEGO PRESSED AGAINST THE TREE, WISHING HIS HEART WASN'T pounding so loudly.

He'd lost the soldier. He hadn't heard anything for a few minutes now, which had to mean that G.I. Joe had given up his search and was heading back to the camp for dinner.

So why was Diego still frozen in place?

Because that soldier had been a bundle of nerves. Voice quivering. Weapon cocked. Gun wavering in the air. Way too close to firing. Diego closed his eyes, but all he could see were the cold black barrels of that rifle.

Opening his eyes again, he took a deep breath, taking in the dappled sunlight, the brush, the branches waving in the light October breeze. So calm.

How long had he been sitting here, hiding here?

It felt like an hour. If the soldier was still around, he would have made his attack by now, right?

Right. Diego stood up, listening for the sound of a human in the forest.

Nothing. Nothing but the gentle rattle of leaves stirring in the breeze. He was ready to go find those supplies he'd buried twenty paces from the dry creek bed.

He stepped into a clearing, near the tall oak he'd once used as a target for archery practice with his friends. He could remember Billy Jenner, always taunting him about the way he squinted when he aimed.

Crack.

A rush of adrenaline shot through Diego as he recognized the sound of a rifle being cocked. He spun and saw the soldier, gun trained on him, barely fifteen feet away.

"You're right in my sights, man," the soldier said. "Put the gun down and cut this crap."

Diego's heart was thumping so hard, he couldn't stay still. He thundered across the clearing and plunged into the shadow of trees on the other side. The rifle bounced wildly at his side, a leaden weight that struck his hip bone with a *thwack* every other step.

He reached for it, meaning to hold it still, knowing he should throw it off so it wouldn't slow him down, but he wasn't willing to give it up. It was his, damn it, and he needed it—especially now.

"Stop or I'll shoot!" the soldier yelled after him.

Diego's pulse was so loud in his ears, he barely

heard. There was only the hammer of his heartbeat, the thump of his feet on the ground.

Then a sickening, loud blast followed by almost immediate pain. White-hot pain tearing through his left leg.

He shot me! Diego stumbled, gasping, as the bullet burned through his skin, through the pumping muscle of his thigh.

"I said stop! What the hell's the matter with you?" The soldier was screaming now.

You shot me, Diego thought. *You actually shot me.*

With the bitter surge of nausea and the fire in his thigh, Diego could no longer run, but he refused to turn back and surrender to that bastard. He stumbled and limped, each step on his left leg producing a jagged arc of pain.

The dry creek bed loomed ahead of him, but there was no chance of jumping. No way across.

He teetered on the edge of the embankment, wavering from the dizzying pain that screamed through his leg. He drew in a shaky breath, trying to calm down, but suddenly the trees above him were spinning, and the sky was dark and the pain was too much.

SEVEN

WHEN THE GUNSHOT EXPLODED IN THE SILENCE OF THE forest, Irene Margolis fell behind a tree and froze.

Oh my God, oh my God. Her brain seemed as paralyzed as the rest of her body, the words echoing through her mind like the shot through the forest.

A gunshot. What did it mean? Well, most importantly, that there was another person nearby—someone besides herself and Aaron and Dad out here in the Big Empty. Certainly not their guide. So far none of the Novo Mundum contacts had carried weapons; violence just wasn't what the place was about.

Another person . . . and a gunshot.

Whatever it added up to, Irene had a dread feeling it couldn't be good.

Then she heard the crunch of leaves . . . something was moving through the dry brush just a few yards away.

Holding her breath, she dared to peer around the fat tree trunk. On the opposite bank of the dry creek stood a soldier—a young man in a helmet and speckled green fatigues. He held a rifle loosely in one hand, and he was staring down into the ravine.

Following his gaze, Irene saw a body sprawled among the stones and leaves in the dry riverbed.

"Oh my God." Her lips moved against her palm. It was foolish to even breathe this close to the soldier, but she couldn't help herself.

Someone was shot. The soldier had shot someone.

He eased down into the dry creek. "Don't move!" he shouted, tentatively edging closer to the body. When he extended his rifle, Irene braced herself for another shot, but instead the soldier nudged the body.

A poke at the shoulder.

Barrel into the abdomen.

The soldier shook his head. He scrambled up the shallow trench, looked around him, then headed off.

Irene stared ahead at the body, stunned. Was he dead? Or so badly hurt the soldier hadn't thought he could do anything?

After the soldier had been gone for a minute or two, Irene stepped over the large stones. Her eyes fixed on the frighteningly still body—a blur of khaki green T-shirt and worn jeans. The skin was pale, but the chest seemed to be rising slightly, breathing.

She dropped to her knees, clenching her shaking

hands against her chest. There was no time to panic, not if he'd been shot.

Shot. "Oh my God," she whispered again as she took in his face—dark brow and dark, glossy hair. A teenage boy.

"Hey," she whispered, gently shaking his shoulder. "Can you hear me?"

No response. He was unconscious. Okay, next step.

He was faceup, more or less, so she started with what she knew from the first aid class she'd taken. "ABC," she said softly. "Airway, breathing, circulation."

Two fingers under his chin. Other hand on his forehead. She tilted his head back, then leaned down to listen for breathing. His chest rose and fell a little erratically, but he was definitely breathing and his throat seemed clear.

Two fingers against his neck. She searched for the carotid artery and found it, a steady beat beneath the skin.

"A solid pulse," she murmured. "That's good."

She knew she shouldn't move him. If he'd fallen down into the riverbed, he could have broken bones or a spinal injury. And he'd been shot, right? She had heard a gunshot.

If that was the source of his injury, Irene had to find the bullet wound—now. No ambulance was going to come screeching up to take him away out here in the woods, in the middle of the Big Empty.

She sat back and ran her hands lightly over his chest and arms, feeling for a wound. Just dirt and leaves. But as she knelt closer, she realized the leaves beneath him were shiny with something dark. Blood.

Gently she lifted the leg and lowered her head to look at it. The back of his jeans was slimy with the wet, red stuff, pumping from a singed hole in the fabric.

A bullet in his leg—his left thigh. Only an entry wound, so the bullet had to be lodged there.

Her brain clicked into action, trying to picture the illustrations in her anatomy book, the one she'd practically memorized, luckily, because of her fascination with medicine. She winced as the image came to her— the femoral artery was right there, possibly in the direct path of the bullet.

That was *so* bad. If the artery had been hit, he would bleed out in the next minute.

If not, there was a chance he might live, as long as she could stop the bleeding.

She slid her hands beneath him and heaved, rolling him onto his stomach, immediately bearing down on the wound as hard as she could with the heels of both hands.

"Stop bleeding," she whispered. "Come on." The blood was warm and wet and incredibly pungent. She'd watched all the trauma shows and reruns of *ER* for years, and the sight of it didn't bother her, but feeling it . . . She shuddered. Somehow the warm stickiness got to her.

"Irene!"

She whipped her head around and saw her father and older brother, Aaron, running toward her. Shaking her head, she hissed, "Quiet! There was a soldier. . . . He may be nearby."

"What happened?" her father asked.

"I don't know," she said over her shoulder. "But this guy was shot, and then this soldier was poking at him and . . ." She looked up at her father, whose face was shockingly pale in the gloom. "I think the soldier *shot* him, Dad."

"Maybe the kid shot someone first," Aaron said. He slid a sneakered foot toward the other side of the boy's body, and Irene looked up to see something she hadn't noticed in her haste to check him over—a rifle slung from a worn canvas strap.

"Maybe he was hunting?" she said.

Aaron narrowed his eyes.

"Aaron, he could die!" Irene said. "If he doesn't stop bleeding, he will."

With that, she lifted her hands away to see if the blood flow had slowed.

"Oh no." Her hands were soaked. The blood was still pumping steadily from the wound, and if it didn't stop soon, he was gone. She felt a wave of dizziness pass over her, staring at her hands with his blood all over them.

This was his life, her call.

"He's bleeding too much," her father said, kneeling beside her. "What can we do?"

"I . . . I don't know." Irene jammed her hands against the raw flesh again, trying to think. The boy's face was grey now. He was losing too much blood, too fast.

"Take the bullet out," Aaron said, leaning over to squint at the boy's leg. "That's what's causing the bleeding, right?"

"We can't!" She shook her head. "It might be near the femoral artery. The really big one," she explained when she saw Aaron's frown. "If I got anywhere near that or if the bullet moved while I was trying to . . . *No.* I just have to stop the bleeding. Somehow."

A memory of one of the medical shows she'd often watched flashed through her head. *Elevation.* That might work. And while she was at it, she could apply pressure to the pulse point below his hip bone. If she cut the blood supply off farther up . . .

"What are you doing?" Aaron said, kneeling as she rolled the boy over again.

"Lifting his leg. It makes it harder for the blood to flow." Hooking the boy's knee over her shoulder, she bent low and pressed the heel of her hand into the web of muscle just below his hip bone.

"Give me . . . I don't know, your T-shirt. Something," she said to her brother. "I need to soak some of this up."

Aaron raised his arms and stripped off his old grey Liberty Prep gym shirt. Irene lifted her hands while he jammed the wadded fabric beneath the boy's bloody thigh.

Within seconds the pale cotton was soaked deep red.

"It's not helping," Irene said. Biting her lower lip, she pressed harder, her mind racing. There was only one other thing to try—a tourniquet.

It was risky. She'd seen an episode of an emergency medicine show once where they talked about how modern paramedics avoided using tourniquets because of the damage to the body's circulation. If she left it on too long and cut off all the blood to his leg, the flesh would start to die and he would probably lose his leg at some point.

But if she didn't try it, he would die.

She glanced up at her father and brother, thinking how ironic it was that she felt so unprepared for a moment like this. She, the girl who'd always said she wanted to be a doctor, who watched *Trauma: Life in the ER* every chance she got, the student who volunteered at the hospital and read medical textbooks each night in bed.

Her father's eyes were full of turmoil as he asked, "Irene, what do you want to do?"

She took a deep breath, then answered, "I don't think we have a choice."

EIGHT

"MICHAEL, SLOW DOWN!" MAGGIE CRIED.

Michael banged into the tile wall of the subway corridor as he turned to face her. During the long ride into Brooklyn on the C train he'd had time to think things over, devise a plan, even if it was a short-term escape. Maggie had been grateful for a chance to rest her feet, so grateful that she'd clammed up for a while, which was fine with Michael. If he heard her complain about those damned shoes one more time, he was going to toss them into the East River.

"Just wait," Maggie moaned. She was doubled over, hands on her thighs, panting. "I can't . . . keep up . . . with you."

Worried that they'd be spotted by passing cops or

soldiers, he pulled her into the shadowed doorway of a boarded-up underground shop. "You have to keep going, Maggie." His voice was stern, trying to connect with the lost soul behind those stormy eyes. "Think about it. Henry knows us, and there was that other witness. Anyone could give the police our names, our descriptions."

She shook her head, her eyes glistening with tears. "But I didn't do—"

"I know," he said, more gently this time. "I didn't do anything either, but Henry doesn't believe that. And if cops take his word over ours, we're dead. We can't risk it."

He put his arm around her shoulders and pulled her against him, which seemed to make her feel worse. She sucked in a breath and began sobbing. Hot, wet tears rolled down her cheeks, dropping onto his T-shirt. He wanted to growl at her not to be so dramatic, but the truth was, for once she had a right to be.

Once there would have been an easy fix. A heart-to-heart with Dad. A phone call to someone in the district attorney's office. Maybe two calls, max. Not that Michael had ever been in trouble before, but everybody who was anybody in New York knew Graham Bishop, if only because he'd provided the security for their apartments and penthouses. He was a self-made success, with plenty of money to prove it, and that used to make a difference in this city.

It didn't now. The government and the military had all the power, and there wasn't the time or the resources to sort through extenuating circumstances.

These days if you broke the law, you paid with your life. No questions asked, no excuses. Forget about Miranda rights and trials with high-priced defense teams, forget about surviving if you got on the wrong side of the government.

"Come on," Michael said, taking Maggie's hand. "We've got to get out of here."

"Like we're going to be any safer up on the street?" She pulled her hand away. "We can't just keep running, and we've reached the end of the subway line. There are cops in Brooklyn too."

"We're not staying in Brooklyn, not if I can help it."

Maggie swiped her cheeks with the backs of her hands. "What's that mean? Where are we going?"

"Our warehouse is half a mile from this subway stop. It'll take some finagling, but if I can make a deal with the dispatcher, we might be able to catch a ride in the back of a truck going cross-country."

Maggie scowled at him. "Are you insane? You want us to drive out to the Big Empty in the back of a dusty old truck? People die in the backs of trucks, Michael. And the Big Empty is totally deserted now. It's not safe."

Michael crossed his arms, annoyed. Suddenly she was concerned about safety? "Well, it's not safe to stay here either."

Her bottom lip pushed out in a pout. "Can't we go to your place? Your father can fix everything, right?"

He felt his teeth grind. "Don't you get it? This is beyond him. Beyond anybody we know. Sorry if you missed it, but we're under martial law, and they're trying to make an example out of people who are stupid enough to commit violent crimes."

"Are you calling me stupid?"

"Two kids were executed for stealing a few batteries. What do you think they'll do to kids who stole a week's worth of essentials coupons and whacked a shop owner on the back of his head?"

That seemed to get Maggie's attention. She slumped against the wall.

"We'd better get moving," Michael said, checking his watch. It was nearly seven, and the truck usually left by eight.

Saying it aloud suddenly made it real, even more real than running for blocks until his lungs were burning or jumping at the screech of police sirens. They were going to have to leave Manhattan with the clothes on their backs and whatever was in their pockets. Without a good-bye to his father or anyone else he knew. This was the ultimate "What five things would you grab in a fire?" scenario, and he was walking away with zero, thanks to his girlfriend. Who was supposed to have been history by now.

He looked toward the staircase, now grey with receding sunlight. "Let's go. I've got to negotiate something with the truck driver, and we'll need some food and water and things. Probably some shoes you can walk in."

"But Michael . . ."

If she said that one more time, his head was going to explode. "We don't have a choice," he said, his too-loud voice echoing in the hollow corridor. He took a breath, then moved closer to add: "The police *will* find us in New York. Unless we're not here to be found."

"Okay." She stepped forward and linked her arm through his. They started up the stairs into a street that used to bustle with pedestrians and vendors with push-carts.

This is our only choice, our only escape.

Even as he told himself that, Michael couldn't stop the fresh surge of frustration in his gut. He hadn't signed on for any of this—not the virus, not the girl-friend who'd turned into a basket case, none of it. But that didn't make a damn bit of difference now.

He was headed to the Big Empty, running for his life, running *from* his life, with no return in sight.

NINE

"HOW LONG HAS IT BEEN NOW?" IRENE SHOT THE QUESTION AT her brother.

"Ten minutes." Aaron stared at her over the boy's body. "Is that long enough?"

How do I know for sure? Irene wondered as her fingers tested the skin of his leg—not grey yet, which was good. She knew that even experienced doctors found it difficult to make the call on how long to leave a tourniquet on. And the consequences could be huge. If she left the tourniquet on too long, the lack of oxygen to the limb would destroy his leg. It was a lot better than dying, of course . . . but she wanted this kid to live *with* his leg. Whole and healthy, the way he'd been before he was shot.

"Eleven minutes," Aaron said. "Take it off, Reenie. You said you wanted to take it off after ten. That's long enough, right?"

"I hope," she said, biting her bottom lip. "I mean, they make this look so easy on the medical shows, but when it comes down to trying to save someone's life in the woods . . ."

"Irene." She felt her father's hand on her shoulder, a familiar, comforting weight. "We know you're doing your best."

"Right." She stared at the boy's leg in the fading light. Had the wound stopped bleeding?

Tentatively she slid her fingers over the makeshift bandage. It was stiff with dried blood. She found the knot and worked it loose, bending low to see any fresh spurts.

Her hands started to shake as she saw the results. No new blood—no new blood! There was no fresh flow there, only the warm, sticky remains of the previous bleeding. The blood had clotted.

She squeezed her eyes shut against a surge of adrenaline. Relief actually had a taste, metallic and sharp.

"He's okay?" her dad asked, squatting beside her. "Irene?"

"I think so." Her voice was steady. "I think we did it."

She arranged herself cross-legged beside the boy and reached for his hand. Feeling his pulse—thready and weak as it was—was a comfort, though she couldn't help but flash back to the report of the soldier's rifle.

That thundering shot. The retreating soldier. The

sight of the kid's still body. It was all finally hitting her. Why was this boy out here with a gun? And what kind of soldier would shoot a teenager?

Of course, the people at Novo Mundum had warned them that the military was taking the Big Empty's evacuation seriously. For Irene that had meant getting past the border patrols safely and not much else. Despite their guide's warning, she was shocked by the shooting, shocked that someone could be shot just for being in the E Zone. Unless . . . Was this guy one of those dangerous rebels she'd heard rumors about? She looked at his sleeping face, so peaceful and sweet. Her heart gave a gentle tug—somehow she couldn't believe that was true.

Maybe being out here was more risky than they'd realized when they decided to travel to Novo Mundum. She'd imagined various adventures when she had agreed to make this journey with her father and brother, but none of the wildest scenarios she'd come up with had included random violence.

"So what now?" Aaron asked, jarring her out of her thoughts. He straightened up and jammed his hands in his pockets.

"We need to get back to the campsite," their father said. "It's going to get cold when the sun goes down."

"We can't just leave him here," Irene protested.

Her father scratched his beard. "Reenie, we can't carry him that far."

"Then let's bring the campsite here," Irene said. "We'll need the sleeping bags and some firewood and—"

"You're forgetting one big problem." Aaron raised his eyebrows. "This kid came from somewhere. Probably nearby, since he wasn't carrying any rations or supplies. Unless we find a backpack tossed in the bushes, I'd say he's got a clan. Or a gang."

"Aaron, look at him," Irene argued. "He's not going anywhere. I'll wait with him."

"Aaron's right. I don't want to leave you here if someone's coming to get him," her father countered.

"Come on, Dad. I'll be okay, really. You heard the shot, so you'll hear me scream if anything . . ." She trailed off at the look of alarm on her father's face. "Not that anything else is *going* to happen. It's quiet, right? Has been for a while now."

Aaron picked up the boy's rifle and checked it over. "Not army issue. More like a hunting rifle, but that doesn't mean he's not one of those renegade gangs. Remember what the last guide told us about the—what was it, the Slashers? They're trouble. They kidnap people—and worse."

Irene dropped to her knees once again and leaned over the unconscious boy. She vigorously rubbed her knuckles over his clavicle bone.

"What are you doing?" Aaron asked.

"I'm going to wake him up," she answered. "I've seen this on medical shows. I'm going to wake him up and get some answers so you'll let me stay with him."

Aaron stepped away and kicked at some leaves. "Great. Let me make sure his rifle is out of reach so he doesn't shoot us all."

The boy didn't react, so she persisted, jiggling her knuckles against the base of his throat. That prompted a moan. His face tensed, dark eyebrows creasing.

"I think he's coming out of it," she said, leaning closer. "Can you hear me? Tell me your name."

He stirred again, his head falling to one side and his eyelids fluttering. She brushed his dark hair off his forehead. "Tell me your name," she whispered into his ear. "Who are you?"

"Dee-uh," he croaked. "Dee . . . Diego."

"That's your name? Diego?" She patted his shoulder gently.

He nodded, wincing with pain. "He shot me," he breathed in disbelief.

"I know, I know, but we're taking care of you, Diego," Irene said, looking across to her father. "You're going to be okay. Everything will be fine. But you need to tell us where you came from. Is someone going to be looking for you? Missing you?"

"No," he breathed. "No one. They all died."

Irene shook her head. "Then how did you get out here all alone?" she asked. He was fading, so she pressed her knuckles to his collarbone and rubbed again. "Tell us, Diego. Where did you come from?"

"The farm . . . my grandmother's farm." His voice was a weak whisper.

"Where?" Aaron asked. "Is it close?"

"A mile. Across the clearing. Turn left at the bull's-eye."

"He lives here," her father said, his voice tinged with

disbelief as he glanced toward the clearing. He straightened and scratched his beard. "Well, that settles it."

"I'm not leaving him," Irene insisted.

"You don't have to," her father said. "If the farm is that close, we'll have a place to spend the night. You stay here with him while Aaron and I go on ahead. With luck, we'll be back with something to cart him home in within the hour."

Aaron hitched Diego's rifle over his shoulder. "Don't talk to any strangers," he joked as he backed away.

"Don't worry," she whispered, smoothing back Diego's hair. Funny how she'd only just stumbled on his body in the woods but she already felt connected to him. Committed. "We'll get you home. I promise."

TEN

As Keely's bike rolled through the gates of Griffith Park, she felt a wave of that eerie sense of isolation that often hit her since Strain 7. The deserted park looked like an untouched wilderness, its grass grown tall and gone to seed, waving gently in the warm breeze. The fence that enclosed it was covered with a solid blanket of scarlet bougainvillea, and the only sound came from birds chirping in the trees. Paradise.

The image didn't quite work, though, with the giant military tank situated right outside the entrance. Tanks were everywhere these days, and usually Keely barely noticed them—they blended into the streets so naturally. But here at the park, the tank's presence was still jarring.

Strange how it felt good to be unsettled by the sight.

At least a part of her still hadn't fully accepted what life in America had become.

Keely climbed off her bike, sweating, and lifted her heavy ponytail from the back of her neck. With private cars outlawed to preserve fuel and all of L.A. biking and walking everywhere, no one bothered to exercise for the hell of it. Gone were the joggers and tai chi classes and young mothers pushing running strollers. You burned calories just trying to get anywhere, and why go for a romp in the fresh air when the fresh air could kill you?

Coasting on one pedal, Keely started down the path toward the carousel. With a shortage of resources, the merry-go-round was out of service. Keely passed the boarded-up ticket booth and circled around the carousel, looking for Von. A young, tired-looking dad was sitting on the merry-go-round's scuffed floor while a little girl climbed on and off the horses frozen in midair.

Could he be Von? Making contact with his kid in tow? Keely squinted at him, debating. She didn't have a good feeling about approaching a strange man like that, even with the little girl there. If that was Von, maybe she'd have to drop this plan and head home. She was living dangerously here, but her gut told her to stay away from any guy who'd drag his kid into an e-mail relationship.

Then Keely spotted a girl sitting on a bench, not much older than herself. She was reading a book. Keely wheeled toward her, trying to seem casual.

The girl lowered the book and Keely noticed the title. *Today's Child.*

Contact.

The girl smiled as Keely's bike squeaked to a stop beside the bench. She raised her fingers to her chin, and Keely returned the gesture.

"Keely?" The girl set her book down, shielding her eyes from the sun with one hand.

"Yeah." Keely realized her heart was pounding. A leftover effect of the long bike ride or simple nerves?

"I'm Ineo." The girl's brown hair was short and it feathered out in a cute way, reminding Keely of a baby duck.

"Ineo," Keely said aloud, realizing it was the one part of the previous message she hadn't been able to decode.

"I'm glad you decided to meet me," Ineo said.

"I was curious." Keely propped her bike against the back of the bench and sat, one knee propped up so she could face Ineo. "The puzzles and codes you sent really hooked me."

"Actually, those weren't from me," Ineo replied. "But I'll explain that in a minute. You're good with cryptology—lots of people we contact don't have the first clue how to figure out our messages."

"Lots of people"—so this really was something big. Keely had known that, deep down, but it was a relief to hear the words. Now she just needed to know more.

"It wasn't that hard, really." Keely shrugged. "I used to go to Knightsbridge Academy," she went on, not sure how much to say. That Knightsbridge was a progressive school with a program for gifted kids? That she missed the challenge? That she'd been taking AP college classes as a sophomore, on track for early admission to USC before the virus had cut the heart out of her plans?

"I know all that," Ineo said. "The e-mails that were sent to you weren't a coincidence. Novo Mundum chose you, Keely. They value your intellect and initiative. They asked me to meet you in person because it's my job to recruit exceptional people like you."

Keely felt a flutter of panic mixed with excitement. "Recruit?" She swallowed. "So who, where . . . I mean, what *is* Novo Mundum?"

"I guess we're doing a good job of keeping it secret," Ineo said with an easy smile. "We chose the name Novo Mundum because it actually means "I make the world anew." We're a community, and we're dedicated to working hard to rebuild our lives, to create a safe, comfortable place to live. A place where we can achieve not only basic comforts, but also intellectual fulfillment."

"Like—like a utopian society?" Keely asked, taking in a sharp breath.

Ineo laughed. "Honestly, we both know the human condition doesn't allow utopia. But on a good day, I'd say Novo Mundum comes pretty close. We grow our own fruits and vegetables, take care of cows and chickens to provide eggs, milk, and meat. We all look out for each other in an environment of understanding rather than rules. And we haven't lost sight of all the greater reasons for life that seem to have vanished in the rest of the world—the beauty of words, music, art. Those priorities still exist for us at Novo Mundum. We know the soul needs nourishment as much as the body needs it."

Keely shook her head. "How do you do it? How do you get around the government regulations and rules?"

"It hasn't been a major problem for us, but then, we're operating pretty far away from government enforcement."

Pretty far away . . . "You mean, in the Big Empty?"

Ineo nodded.

"Wow." Keely sat back, reeling. So Chris had been right, sort of. There *was* life out there—much better than the life they had here in Los Angeles, it sounded like. She studied Ineo's clear, pale eyes. "Sorry if I seem shocked, but this is all so unreal."

"Oh, we're real, all right."

"And defying the law . . ."

"Kind of like the men who fought the American Revolution," Ineo said. "It's a good thing Paul Revere and Patrick Henry weren't afraid to stand up for liberty and freedom. We're not waiting around for MacCauley or his board to reorganize the masses. We're rebuilding from the ground up, tending to physical, emotional, and intellectual recovery. We're pooling our resources, which include some of the finest minds of this century."

Keely gazed out at the trees as it began to sink in. Novo Mundum was a real place—a community—and they wanted her to join them. Kind of a modern take on *Little House on the Prairie,* she thought, picturing herself as a pioneer in a new frontier, a world that would replace everything she'd lost when her life shattered into a million pieces. Inside her, hope flickered.

"Too much to process?" Ineo asked.

"No, not at all, it's just . . ." Keely shrugged. "Call me a skeptic, but it sounds too good to be true. What else can you tell me? How did Novo Mundum start?"

"Let's see. . . . The community was actually started by a biochemist." Ineo lowered her voice. "He was conducting research before the virus hit, and now he's working on an antidote to prevent this nightmare from ever happening again."

Like her mother. Epidemiology had been Mom's specialty before Strain 7. With the shortage of doctors now, she had to pitch in wherever she could, whether she was setting a broken bone or removing an appendix, but viruses were what she knew. How they behaved, how they mutated, how they spread. Keely's mind raced, thinking of being at her mom's side at Novo Mundum, working to build a better society.

"You can join us, Keely," Ineo said. "You can make a difference. Everything you need is there—food, housing, medical care, even a top-notch education. We've got last year's Pulitzer Prize–winner teaching poetry, as well as philosophers, writers, scholars. It would be a perfect fit for you. A place to grow."

"I want to go," Keely said. "I'd really like to. But I just . . . I don't know." As amazing as it all sounded, it was also terrifying to think of actually defying the law and journeying into the abandoned zone. Keely, the girl who'd never so much as turned in a late assignment in her old life.

Even if she really could bring herself to break the law, she'd heard so many rumors about what was left out there—decaying remains of Strain 7 victims in abandoned towns, rebels waiting to terrorize you for kicks, and soldiers armed and ready to kill anyone at first sight, no questions asked.

Ineo made Novo Mundum sound incredible, but how far could Keely trust her? How could she know this was all true, that it was worth taking so many huge risks?

"Why don't you take some time to think about it," Ineo said, "because we need a commitment. As you can imagine, getting to Novo Mundum is challenging, and we don't have the resources to waste on someone who's unsure."

"That makes sense," Keely said. She frowned. "Let me ask you, is everyone recruited? I mean, could I come with my mother? She's also an immunologist, and . . . well, I think she could use the break."

Ineo nodded. "I'm aware of her background. I'm sure we could use her help if she's interested. But don't reveal any facts of our existence until you're sure. Can you just feel her out about it?"

Keely nodded. "No problem. I can be subtle."

Ineo touched her fingertips to her chin and smiled. "We'll be in touch, then."

Keely felt a smile tug at her lips as she hopped on her bike. Suddenly the park didn't seem so bleak and empty. Maybe life was going on out there after all—somewhere in the Big Empty—and it was good.

Almost utopia.

ELEVEN

As the bus rolled north up Interstate 75, Amber twisted toward the window and wondered if the woman in the next seat would ever shut up. She tried to focus on the passing landscape, but the black, charred orange groves were only a reminder of the hellish world that had taken over after Strain 7. The riots and local revolts, the looting and vandalism—all the charming ways that people had decided to destroy their neighborhoods before the virus destroyed them. The sight of burnt tree nubs and ashen plots of dirt made her more nauseous than ever, and she ran a hand over her forehead, wiping off the beads of sweat.

"Are you all right, dear?" asked her seatmate.

"Just tired," Amber said, wishing the woman weren't so enamored of her.

Amber had made it onto the bus in style, with the driver even announcing that she was freaking Faith Stank, board member Stank's daughter. He'd seemed a little put out by her ancient T-shirt, faded cotton hoodie, and ripped cargo pants, but what did he know? Anyway, the stir about the board member's daughter had rippled through the passengers, right back to "Faith's" assigned seat beside the old lady Amber had met in the bathroom.

No perfect theft goes unpunished, Amber thought, trying not to sigh aloud as Thelma Appelman prattled on about her nephews whose mommy was gone. Tuning her out, Amber stared out at passing palm trees. She was wondering whether the bus driver might get a radio call about Faith's stolen backpack when Thelma blinked in her face.

"What was that?" Amber asked, realizing she'd missed the question.

"I was just wondering, Faith—what takes you to New Orleans?" Thelma asked as she pulled a ball of yarn, knitting needles, and a splotch of knitting out of her bag.

"A . . . friend," Amber said, realizing this woman wouldn't give up until she'd gotten an earful. "She's having a hard time, and I'm going to help her."

"School troubles?"

"Not exactly." Amber glanced up into the old woman's eyes. They were the color of old denim, patient eyes. Okay. If Granny wanted a story, Amber would let it rip.

"She's all alone now since the virus. Used to live

with her mom, who waited tables in a diner, but she's dead now. So, my friend—her name's Amber—well . . ."

"Is probably lonely and frightened," Thelma said gently. "It must be terrifying to go through all of this so young and all by herself."

"She can totally take care of herself," Amber argued. "I mean, her mom was cool and all, but Amber never, like, depended on her, if you know what I mean."

"I see." Thelma nodded, her eyes on her knitting.

"So Amber met this guy—Carter. He was kind of cute, with mysterious grey eyes and dark hair he wore in a ponytail and . . ." She trailed off, picturing his face.

Carter Hobbes. His name sounded like something straight out of a PBS special—"upper crust," her mom would have called it. But Carter was nothing like that, with his glossy hair and the trio of earrings in his left ear. He was cool—or he had been, at first.

"She just fell for him, you know?" Amber said, staring at the strands of purple and green yarn inching through Thelma's needles. "They hung out, and she figured that was better than being alone. It wasn't like she, you know, really cared about him or needed him there or anything. And then . . . they did more than hang out. She kind of moved in with him, and that was okay. He was alone too. But then—then she got pregnant." Amber paused, checking Thelma's expression for distaste or disapproval, but Thelma seemed cool with that. "So she told him, and he flipped." She shrugged, ignoring the familiar stab of hurt and rage she'd felt when she discovered he was gone.

It wasn't all her fault that she'd gotten pregnant. And it wasn't like she'd had some kind of huge white-picket-fence fantasy or something. She just hadn't thought he'd really . . . leave.

Ugh. The whole scenario reeked like some lame cable movie, with a weepy teenage heroine and her no-good weasel of a boyfriend.

She *could* take care of herself, that was the thing. She always had, even when her mom made those weak efforts to hang around at home with her instead of going off with some new boyfriend.

Amber could survive. But taking care of a baby . . . that was a whole different survival story. Especially now. Babies ate Cheerios and crackers and other stuff Amber wasn't too sure about, but definitely not protein shakes and synthetic power bars that tasted like ground-up cardboard mushed together with honey and Elmer's glue.

But Carter didn't care about that, obviously. Carter only cared about one thing—himself. Well, that would change.

Just as soon as Amber caught up with him.

TWELVE

KEELY TWISTED THE KNOB TO THE BACK DOOR, SURPRISED TO see a light on in the kitchen. It was just one lonely bulb over the sink, but it was more than usual. It meant her mom was actually home for the first time in days.

A hospital ID badge lay on the counter: CATHERINE GILMORE, M.D., was printed beneath a picture taken long before Strain 7, showing Keely's mom holding back a surprised laugh at something the photographer had said. The photo seemed wrong somehow, probably because it had been a long time since Keely had seen Mom smile.

She kicked her sneakers off in the doorway, sniffing the air. Instant mashed potatoes, the kind that came in a box and were sent into space on the shuttles. Not

Keely's favorite meal, but nobody could be picky any-more. She spotted the pan on the stove and peeked under the lid. Empty.

"Mom?" she called.

There was no answer, but Keely could hear the faint murmur of TV voices from the family room. "Mom?" she called again, dropping her backpack on the kitchen floor.

"Keely?"

Why did her mother sound so surprised? Keely still lived here, or had Mom forgotten that? Walking into the den, Keely noticed the small bowl of potatoes in her mother's hands. Dinner for one.

Like Keely didn't even exist.

"What are you doing home?" her mother asked, blinking up at her from the meager glow of a lamp on the table next to the couch, where she was curled up in sweats and a T-shirt.

Keely stared back at her, dumbfounded. How could she say that when Keely sat around night after night waiting for her mother to show up and usually going to bed alone in the dark, long after lights-out curfew? When Keely woke up in the morning to find the meals she had left for her mother stale and crusty on the kitchen table?

And when Keely had just spent the hour's ride back from Griffith Park picturing the relief on her mother's face when Keely told her about Novo Mundum, about the difference she could make there, about the chance for the two of them to reconnect and start over instead of passing each other in this hollow, echoing house, where every room held memories of Dad and Bree.

"I live here, Mom," she said finally, choking back a lump of emotion. "Did you forget that? I'm here all the time. By myself. I don't have a convenient escape hatch like you."

Catherine leaned over to set the bowl on the coffee table, her shoulders stiff, her mouth set in a tight line. "I don't know what you mean by an escape hatch, Keely. I work at the hospital, not a day spa."

Keely shut her eyes as she dropped into the over-stuffed chair across from her mother. "And you have to be there twenty-four-seven, right?"

Catherine stood up and pressed a hand to her forehead. "I'm too exhausted to get into an argument now."

"Are you too exhausted to read my notes, Mom?" Keely jumped up and pushed past her mother to reach the door to the fridge. She snatched the stack from the magnet and turned around to wave them at Catherine. "Do you ever notice that I try to let you know where I am, when I'll be home? Do you even care?"

"You're acting like a child, Keely." Catherine folded her arms over her chest and stared at the ceiling with exasperation. "You don't have any idea what I do all day or what I'm trying to do when I'm not down in the ER working like a slave."

"So why don't you tell me, Mom?" Keely shouted, blinking back the tears that flooded her eyes. "I want to know! At least then maybe I'd believe you remember I'm around. I'm the one who *didn't* die, you know?"

Sudden spots of color burned Catherine's pale cheeks, and her mouth had hardened into a slash of fury. "I'm going to bed now," she said, her voice like steel. Then she turned and walked up the stairs, her bare feet silent on the carpet.

That was it? Keely wanted to scream. No retort, no reassurance that of course she loved Keely, that she was glad Keely had survived? Nothing.

Slumping into a chair at the kitchen table, Keely buried her hot face in her hands and choked back a sob.

She really wishes I were dead so I wouldn't be around to remind her of Dad and Bree. So she wouldn't have to waste her precious time and energy arguing with me.

And what an idiot I am, expecting Mom to join me at Novo Mundum! Thinking she'd help me figure out whether it's really okay to go and then take me there herself.

Wiping her cheeks with the back of her hand, Keely stood up and went to the desk, where she switched on the computer. She knew there were risks in the decision she was about to make—tons of them. But it wasn't like there was anything in Los Angeles worth holding on to, anyway. Mom had just made it crystal clear—Keely had nothing left to lose.

THIRTEEN

WHEN DIEGO OPENED HIS EYES, THE WORLD WAS BLACK AND cold.

Then he felt the heat, a red fireball of pain in his leg. He tried to swallow, but his mouth was dry and rough inside. He squinted into the darkness, the familiar shapes of the old winterized porch emerging in the night. The fringed lampshade. The television. Nonnie's statue of the Virgin Mary.

The pain flared again and he felt his body tense, bracing against it, fighting it. He saw the soldier's face, his gun wavering in the air, fingers twitching on the trigger. And a surge of pain that made him cry out in the darkness.

"Diego?" a girl's voice chimed. It was followed by

the vision of a pool of candlelight, an angel in its golden ring. "I have something for the pain," the angel said. He watched her mouth move with a kind of fascination. "I found it in your medicine cabinet. You're not allergic to Tylenol with Codeine, are you?"

"No." He tried to sit, but the tug on his leg was excruciating. She pressed the pillow behind him, helping to lift his head. His hand was so shaky, he couldn't hold the cup, but she did it for him. Tucked the pills on the back of his tongue. Pressed the cup to his lips, letting the sweet water pass into his mouth.

Diego swallowed, then felt himself drifting again. His next glimmer of awareness was awash with voices, sounds of fear and strain and anger. Their words floated over him, making perfect sense, yet totally devoid of logic or foundation. Not that it mattered. It was a comfort simply to be in range of human voices.

"I won't leave you behind. You're coming with us," said a gruff voice.

"I won't let him die," the angel replied. "Look, there's no reason for you to miss the meeting with our Novo Mundum contact. Just go, will you? You and Aaron go and make the connection. The guide can send someone back for us later."

The man's voice rose. "I am not going to leave you here alone."

"I'm not alone—I'm with Diego. And I'm not going to leave him now."

Diego felt a fresh breath fill his lungs. His angel was staying with him.

That knowledge was enough to let the voices fade into the oblivion of night.

He heard her move through the room, her footsteps light, tentative. Felt her touch him, her fingertips on his wrist, a damp cloth on his head.

He opened his eyes and saw his mother leaning over him, holding a thermometer, telling him he had to miss school today. That she shouldn't have let him play that soccer game in the rain.

It's okay, Mommy. . . .

Or was it Nonnie? Nonnie passing him the biscuits. Nonnie showing him how to aim the arrow, hold the bow steady before you release and strike!

Mommy, Nonnie, his angel . . . The faces blurred with the pain shooting up his leg, and then he was asleep again.

FOURTEEN

MICHAEL MOVED DOWN THE CENTER OF THE DESERTED CITY street, turning to take in the blue-and-brown-glass sky-scrapers that made up the skyline of Cincinnati. There was a surreal quality to this city, with its glimmering glass storefronts and smoothly paved streets. The white paint in the crosswalk looked clean enough to eat off, and bits of granite sparkled in the immaculate side-walks. It was as if the people of Cincinnati had simply vanished one afternoon, leaving their city clean and neat and totally intact.

"If only they had some people in this damned city," Maggie said, stretching gracefully toward the blue sky overhead.

"This city used to have plenty of people before

MacCauley made it an E Zone," Michael said as he saw his reflection in a plate-glass storefront. Eyes wild, hair spiked up as if he'd stuck his finger in a socket. The look of a fugitive.

Two days ago he'd had a shot at actually meeting the president one day, at holding an important job, possibly in the new government. Now he was running from law enforcement, hiding in the Big Empty.

"How long do we need to stay here?" Maggie asked. "Not that it isn't better than that stuffy truck—oh, man, I can't believe we spent two days in the back of that thing!—but can't we move south and get out of the Big Empty? I used to have an aunt in Dallas. Maybe she's still alive. Or maybe we could move into her place if she's not." She turned and started walking backward in front of Michael. "Texas would be fun, right? We could both get cowboy hats and I could teach you how to ride a horse!"

"Right now we need to find some essentials," Michael said, noticing that this street seemed to end at the waterfront. He wasn't exactly sure what body of water bordered Cincinnati, but he would find out. "And I'll have to get my hands on some maps. But our first priority is survival, and we could probably hole up here for a while if we find some batteries, blankets, and fresh water."

"And food! Something delicious," Maggie said, turning to jog ahead to the water. "And low carb."

"Right," Michael muttered. "Low carb is a top priority." The ironic thing was, when they'd met more than two years ago at a basketball game, Michael had been drawn to Maggie by the way she seemed to pull him out of his rigid, structured, type A approach to life and into someplace looser, softer, more spontaneous. He remembered the first time he saw her, her long, pale blond hair like a swath of silk against her black turtleneck, the silver hoops in her ears flashing at him like a homing signal. Back then, all he'd wanted was to touch her, to keep hearing that wild, carefree laugh. But now everything that had seemed wild and carefree about Maggie had boiled down to a stubborn refusal to accept what had happened to the world. What could happen to her—to *them*.

I've just got to get her to a safe place, Michael thought as Maggie turned down a street that ran along the water—a wide, fast-moving river. Once he had Maggie squared away, he could move on with his life . . . whatever that meant now.

The ringing noise of shattering glass jolted him out of his thoughts. He whirled around to see Maggie standing in front of a hardware store, the pane of its front door lying in jagged pieces on the sidewalk.

"What the hell are you doing?" he shouted.

"I found a crowbar on the street and I tossed it in." She shrugged. "I thought they might have sleeping bags or flashlights inside."

Another case of amazingly poor judgment. Michael gaped at her, not sure what to say.

"What?" she asked.

"Did you have to break the window?"

"Who cares? No one's around."

"Did you ever stop to think the door might be open? The window wasn't even boarded up like the others."

"Again—who cares?" Shaking her head, she reached in to open the door from inside. "We're in Nowheresville, Michael. I don't see why you're so—"

"Shhh!" He held up his hand. "Do you hear that?"

The unmistakable screech of tires, followed by the hum of an engine—an approaching car. "Probably a patrol," Michael whispered, pushing her away from the gaping window. "Come on. We've got to get out of here."

"But this is the Big Empty! Who would be patrolling?"

"Who do you think? Local police, soldiers, whatever they're called out here. They're still evacuating this area, Maggie; it's not a done deal. Whoever it is, I don't want to stick around to find out."

He pulled her to the end of the row of short buildings, then back into an alley. They plunged into the shadows, racing to the alley's end right on the riverfront. Michael quickly absorbed the terrain—the pillars of a squat grey bridge toward the right, a boarded-up pub, scattered benches of a waterfront park, a white stadium looming on the horizon to his left.

"Now what?" Maggie asked. "Can't we go back there and see if—"

A loud squawk interrupted her. "This is the police." The voice came from the other end of the alley—the hardware store. "You are trespassing in an Evacuated Zone. Move to the center of the street with your hands up."

"Oh my God!" Maggie's face crumpled. "I can't believe it. Do we have the worst luck or what?"

"Luck has nothing to do with it when you announce yourself by shattering a window," Michael muttered.

Maggie winced. "I was just trying to help."

He sucked in a breath, calculating their chances of outrunning the police. "Well, we need to leave Cincinnati now, thanks to you."

Maggie glanced behind her. "Can we get back to the trucking center? Maybe on another truck?"

He shook his head. "I've run out of favors. We've got to keep moving." His hand closed around her wrist and he tugged her toward the park.

Behind them the police warning droned on: "I repeat: Move into the street!"

"Where are we going?" she gasped as they clambered behind a field house in the park.

He shielded his eyes from the glare coming off the river. The swift-moving current was evident from the churning surface, swells lapping against the embankment. "Can you swim?"

"In *that* current?"

Michael spotted a ramp at the water's edge. A few feet away stood a low rack of canoes. Six canoes. He'd done his share of paddling at summer camp. "Come on," he said, sliding a fiberglass canoe out of its hold. "We're going on a little cruise."

FIFTEEN

IN A DESERTED BOOTH IN THE SNACK BAR OF THE NEW ORLEANS train station, Amber dug into the first meal she'd had in more than a day—a baked apple. It was soft and seasoned with plenty of cinnamon, and what was best, it was real—actual, straight from the tree.

She scanned the station as she nibbled, looking for Carter. From what she'd been able to figure out on his computer, he was supposed to come through this station sometime this morning and catch the train for Memphis.

That train was leaving in twenty minutes, and she wasn't going to miss him.

She'd never imagined herself chasing after a guy. She wasn't the type to go on one of those talk shows and whine about how much she loved the father of her baby.

No, she didn't want Carter back. She just couldn't stand to let him walk out.

She pushed away the paper bowl with just a few slimy brownish pieces of skin clinging to the sides. Ugh. Eating so fast had been a mistake. Her stomach rolled in protest, but, for the time being, puking didn't seem imminent. She didn't have time to be crouched in a bathroom, anyway. She had to keep a lookout for Carter.

Pulling the heavy backpack over her shoulder, she moved to a seat that allowed her a view of the waiting area. Every other seat was vacant, forming a weird checkered pattern. Strain 7 paranoia. Nobody wanted to sit right next to a stranger, a potential germ sink. The virus had peaked and even receded, but the paranoia lived on.

Amber scanned the vacant faces of the travelers and wondered why Carter would want to go to Memphis. He liked music, but he was never into country. While digging into his computer data, she'd kept seeing the name Novo Mundum, and for a while she'd thought it was a band he was forming. Then she'd realized it was a place, though she wasn't able to find it on a map. She'd even searched for it down in South America, figuring that it sounded like some city in Peru or Brazil. No such luck. Not that his destination really mattered.

It wasn't like she loved him or anything or wanted him back. Finding him was going to serve just one purpose— she had to show him that he'd messed with the wrong girl.

Little Girl. It had been his nickname for her, the one she'd actually used as a Web alias for a while. That would change, really soon.

Hitching up her backpack, she moved toward the rotunda and spotted a sleek black head tilted atop a faded army jacket. Her heart flipped over. Did the jacket have the fierce profile of a crow on the back?

Yes! It was him.

He was way across the waiting room, near the destination and arrival boards, his guitar slung over his shoulder and a stuffed duffel bag at his feet.

She hoisted her backpack and headed across the room, pretending her heart wasn't clanging in her chest like an alarm. *Calm down,* she told herself. *Be cool.*

She walked up behind him and tapped him on the shoulder.

He turned, his grey eyes as pale as she remembered. Recognition dawned there—recognition, then alarm.

"Hey, Carter," she said weakly, hating herself for it.

The silence that followed boomed with tension.

"Carter?" she repeated, feeling her heart kick up again.

"Excuse me?" he said, his voice flat. "I think you . . . uh, have the wrong person." He stepped back.

She lunged forward and grabbed his arm. "What?" she demanded in disbelief. *Is he actually trying to pretend he doesn't know me?* The hurt shot through her but was almost immediately replaced by something much easier—anger. How could he do this to her?

"Look, I'm sorry, but I'm not . . . I mean, I don't

know who Carter is." He wrenched his elbow out of her grasp. "And I don't know who you are."

"Are you kidding me? Are you for real, you piece of—"

A hand was suddenly firm on her elbow. "Is there a problem, miss? Sir?"

She whirled to find a security guard gazing down at her with suspicion, eyebrows beetled together like a hairy centipede. Amber knew she was opening the door to trouble, but she couldn't help herself.

"Oh yeah, there's a problem," she said. "This deadbeat dad is the problem. Are your pals at this mysterious Novo Mundum place in on your scam, Carter?"

"Look." Carter cradled his guitar case, his eyes trained on the guard's like a freaking upstanding citizen. "She thinks she knows me, but she's wrong. I don't know who this little girl is, and I have a train to catch."

Little girl! Amber's teeth clenched. "A train to Novo Mundum, maybe? So you can ditch me and our baby?"

"I don't want trouble here," the security guard said. "How about your ID, miss?"

Carter took that as a cue to take off. Guitar case slamming against his hip, he strode through the waiting room toward the gates.

"Your ID, miss?" the massive security guard prompted.

"Um, sir?" said a girl's voice.

Amber turned to see a teenager behind her. What the hell?

"There's been a mistake," the girl said. "She's with me and I told her to look for my friend, but I guess she found the wrong guy." She turned to Amber. "Didn't I tell you he's tall? And his hair is brown, not black?"

The guard sighed. "Long as there's no more trouble," he said, clearly happy to be rid of them both. "We all got enough of that to go around."

"No more trouble," the girl assured him.

Amber glared at the strange girl. *You got that wrong, sweetie. Butt into my business and your trouble is just beginning.*

SIXTEEN

THE GIRL LOOKED LIKE BREE.

Keely's heart had squeezed as she'd watched the rock star wannabe blow the girl off. She was so young, so clearly in pain, and if the threadbare cargo pants, disheveled blond hair, and puffy eyes were any indication, she was not exactly well cared for. Not unlike a lot of waifs Keely had seen roaming bus stations and train terminals during her trek from L.A. But this girl was different. This girl shared Bree's overwhelming rage.

Then the words *Novo Mundum* had spilled out, and before Keely knew what she was doing, she was tapping on the security guard's arm, lying through her teeth to save the kid's skin. She couldn't let the girl reveal anything about the community, no matter how much pain she was in.

The slight girl's blue eyes tracked the security guard until he disappeared behind a shuttered newsstand. Then she glared at Keely. "Who the hell are you?" she demanded, her voice a rough bark.

"Keely Gilmore," she answered.

"Just what the hell are you doing?"

Well, that didn't sound like Bree at all.

Thinking of Novo Mundum, Keely remembered the code question Ineo had given her. "I've been searching for my father, Albert Camus. Do you know him?"

"Huh?"

Not the answer she was looking for. Keely wasn't sure what to say next. "Never mind," she said. "I was just trying to help. You looked like you needed it."

The girl merely snorted, ripping the hair band out of her scraggly ponytail. Keely noticed her hands shaking as she raked back her hair.

"What's your name?" Keely asked.

"Amber. And no, I'm not twelve. So you can drop the big-sister act right now."

That stung. Amber was so not Bree.

As if to reinforce that, Amber added, "I didn't ask for your help, you know."

"Got that, loud and clear." Keely turned away, then stopped herself. Amber knew something about Novo Mundum, and that something just might help her. Obviously Amber wasn't her guide, but maybe she was also trying to get there and had been given a different code greeting.

Keely turned back around, her heart racing anew. "Novo Mundum. Do you know anything about it?" she asked, motioning Amber toward the wall. They couldn't broadcast the details from the middle of the terminal. In the background a garbled voice on the loudspeaker squawked over the noise of travelers wheeling luggage and the huffing trains down on the platforms. Keely's train to Memphis would be boarding soon, but she could spare this girl a moment or two. "I mean, do you know for sure he's headed there?"

"For all I know, he's headed to Mars on the next space shuttle," Amber said, scowling. "But yeah, from what I figured out, that's where he's going. And I don't know anything except what I picked up from his e-mails."

Keely winced as the picture took focus. So the boyfriend had been recruited, and Amber hadn't. An awkward situation, made worse by Keely stepping in and offering up information just out of pity.

Just because she looks like Bree.

It was time to put all that behind her.

"Um, I actually can't help you," Keely told her. "I thought I could but—"

"Duh! Is this some major power trip for you?" Amber snapped. "You think I can't take care of myself?"

Keely opened her mouth to answer, but Amber didn't give her a chance. "I know your type. You walk around in a straight-out-of-*Vogue* backpack and a shirt your housekeeper ironed before you took off with

Mommy's wallet. And you're in so much pain, right? Poor, poor Keely has it so rough."

The shot hit too close to home. Keely swallowed back the hot, sudden tears that pricked her eyes.

"I don't need your help," Amber said. "So you can just crawl back to your fumigated mansion." She hitched up her packs and marched off, leaving Keely to turn against the wall, trying to hide the flood of pain that had snuck up on her.

So much for being a Good Samaritan. So much for the sisterhood of women, the common bond of rage and pain in the wake of the virus. So much for ever, *ever* again mistaking anyone for the sister she'd lost.

Bree was gone, for real and forever, just like their dad. And dwelling on it—adopting a substitute—was not going to make that fact go away.

All the more reason to move on, to get herself to the next stop on the way to Novo Mundum—Memphis.

With a quick swipe at her wet eyes, Keely adjusted her backpack and strode toward the destination board.

Just a few more minutes and she'd be out of here. Scanning the electronic green lines of print, she found her train.

Train 58 departing at 1:55 PM for Memphis at gate . . .

Her heart sank as the DEPARTED message flashed on the board.

It couldn't be. Her heart hammered as she checked her watch. It was only . . . 1:58?

Oh God.

Turning, she raced toward the platform.

It couldn't be. The train must still be there.

Panting, side aching, she skidded onto the platform and saw the lights of her train shrinking into tiny dots as it disappeared in the tunnel.

Gone. Her next connection to Novo Mundum was gone. She was alone, in a city thousands of miles from home, with only a little money and a ticket and papers for *that* train, not the one tomorrow or the next day. Just another of the government's new ways of restricting everyone to known boundaries, of limiting movement.

"I'm screwed," she said aloud. "Totally screwed."

SEVENTEEN

IRENE'S EYES AND NOSE BURNED FROM THE TANG OF BLEACH AS she leaned over the sink in the kitchen of Diego's farmhouse and scrubbed old T-shirts. After they were rinsed and boiled on the small camp stove, they would make suitable bandages for his wound. So far the area around the bullet's entry didn't seem to be infected, and he had been able to sleep most of the past few days, with the help of the Tylenol with Codeine that Irene had found in the medicine cabinet. She'd spent the last few days drawing on all her medical expertise to figure out how to treat his bullet wound, though nothing could beat good old-fashioned sleep.

Yes, Diego was recovering nicely. She was the one

who couldn't sleep, pacing the halls of this strange, abandoned-looking farmhouse at night.

She twisted a shirt and pushed the curls out of her eyes with the back of her wrist. It didn't help that she'd been a one-person medical team and housekeeper and lookout for four days.

Four days since Dad and Aaron had headed off to meet the guide. Irene was grateful for a roof over her head, but she was too on edge to use the time to rest, with one ear always cocked to hear Diego if he called out, and the vast, empty silence vibrating from beyond the window. She lay in the unfamiliar bed upstairs every night, imagining the reason for every snapped twig or rustle of leaves as the soldier coming to find them, alone here in this echoing farmhouse—a sixteen-year-old girl whose entire knowledge of self-defense hinged on the numbers 9-1-1, and a seventeen-year-old boy with a gunshot wound who was drugged and confined to bed.

She noticed a flurry of motion beyond the kitchen window in her peripheral vision, and her hands froze over the sink. She slowly moved her gaze to see what was out there, shivers traveling down her spine. It was just a squirrel nosing in the garden, scratching at the dirt under the fence with its claws.

Irene sighed with relief, then heard a noise. A soft, shuddering sound, like a whisper . . .

She lifted her head, listening.

"Irene . . ."

Diego. He was awake.

"I'm here!" she called, pressing her gloved hands

into the borrowed apron as she rushed across the living room and into the closed-in porch where he slept.

"Oh my God, you scared me," she told him. "Are you okay? How do you feel?"

"Groggy still. But better." He wrinkled his nose. "You're smelling very . . . clean."

She smiled, stripping off the rubber gloves and letting them fall to the wood floor beside his bed. "Just cleaning up a little. Can I get you something? You must be thirsty."

"I'd like to get out of this bed."

She shook her head emphatically. "No way. If you want to heal properly, you need bed rest. Bad enough your leg got jarred when we carried you back here."

He shook his head. "Luckily I don't remember much of that."

Irene took a pillow from the couch, about to tuck it behind him, but Diego gave her a look that stopped her in her tracks.

"You can stop treating me like a patient. Really. I'm feeling better."

She narrowed her eyes. "Probably those painkillers," she said. "It's a good thing your grandmother had them for her back. But we're almost out. . . ."

"It's fine, I don't need those anymore," he said, lifting a hand to push that thick lock of dark hair from his forehead. "They just make me sleep, anyway. I feel like I've been asleep for a hundred years, like Rumpelstiltskin."

"I think that's Rip van Winkle." Irene reached for the thermometer, giving it a quick shake and then shoving it into his mouth. "And it's only been four days. Well, five if you count that first nightmare of a day."

Diego removed the thermometer. "And no word from your dad?"

She pushed the thermometer back into his mouth, looking away so he wouldn't see the worry in her eyes. "Nothing yet," she answered softly.

"And you can't tell me where they were going?" he mumbled over the thermometer. When she shook her head, he removed it again and held it beyond her reach. "What, were you sworn to secrecy by a group of monks or something? Or no—wait. Your father is a foreign diplomat and he's making arrangements to have the three of you airlifted to, like, Slobovia."

Irene laughed. "Excuse me, but if I were a princess, my country definitely wouldn't have the word *slob* in it."

"Not a princess, a diplomat. It's a liberated fantasy."

"I need to take your temperature."

"It's normal," he said, handing her the thermometer. "See? No flames shooting from my ears."

It felt so good to smile. Diego's sense of humor had been evident almost immediately, but he was definitely much sharper without the painkillers. "Are you hungry?" she asked.

"Always. But I'm really starving for information."

Cocking her head, she sat down on the chair beside the bed. "What? What are you craving to know?"

"All your secrets. Where did your father and brother go? And what were the three of you doing out here in the Big Empty?"

Irene took a deep breath. Really . . . after all they'd been through, she knew Diego wasn't a threat. He could be trusted. "We left Philadelphia to live in Novo Mundum." She waited, watching his reaction for recognition.

He stared back at her blankly. "Where's that? It can't be anywhere around here—I know all the cities for miles."

"It's not exactly a regular city," Irene said. "It's . . . well, it's a place. A special, secret community out here for people who aren't happy with things back at home."

"So your father and Aaron went off to this secret place . . ." he began.

"And they're coming back for us with a guide," Irene told him, thinking back to her last moments with her father. "Just sit tight, sweetie," he'd told her, running his hand through her mess of curls and then crushing her to his chest in a bear hug that nearly broke her ribs. "It's all going to work out."

That was four days ago, and the rendezvous point had been only ten miles north of the campsite they'd set up the night she'd found Diego. Even if Novo Mundum was farther on, which was likely, the guide could have sent her brother back with a message or supplies by now.

But then, they could be on their way to the farmhouse. That was what she told herself at night, lying in bed, her mind racing with possibilities, good and bad.

"And you're worried about them," Diego said, nodding.

"It's only been four days," Irene said, realizing how bad that sounded.

Diego stared back at her, the force of his gaze bringing a deep flush to her neck. She was no actress—she knew he could see how scared she really was. "Do you know where this Novo Mundum place is?" he asked.

"All I know is due north."

He nodded, his dark eyes thoughtful. "Clearwater," he murmured. "It's a small town north of here. I've noticed travelers walking in that direction over the past few months, especially since the evacuation."

"Really . . ." She wondered if Clearwater was Novo Mundum's secret location.

Diego dug his hands into the bed and pushed himself upright, wincing as he gingerly moved his leg. "I'm going to need you to get me some things. Upstairs, in the room with the big old desk. Look in the top right drawer for a bunch of maps."

"Maps?"

"I think we should see if we can pinpoint your promised land."

She shook her head. "They're coming back for us. I know they are."

Diego raised his eyebrows. "I'm sure they're fine," he said. "But if that's really where they went, then we can just find them sooner. Besides, it's no good waiting around here. That soldier is bound to come back, next time with friends."

Irene twisted her hands together, debating the options. As much as she hated to admit it, Diego was right—it was time to move. "The maps," she said at last. "I'll get the maps."

EIGHTEEN

KEELY FELT HER FOOTSTEPS SLOWING AS SHE FOLLOWED HER map through the muggy, tropical streets of New Orleans. What had seemed like a good idea was now getting thorny. As she neared her destination, the charming three-story buildings with wrought-iron balconies looped with ivy were giving way to smaller, flatter homes with blistered paint and broken windows.

So much had changed since Strain 7, but it was still hard not to get creeped out walking through a neighborhood that had clearly not been a good one before the virus. Even after New Orleans was rezoned for the survivors, no one had fixed up the houses here, which meant the area was probably mostly empty.

But this was the best route to the freight terminal,

Keely's brilliant plan B method of transport to Novo Mundum. Passenger trains weren't the only ones still running. Everyone knew that freight trains—now called ghost trains—still carried supplies across the Big Empty. Keely figured that if she found the freight terminal in New Orleans, she could manage to sneak her way onto a ghost train headed north.

North. Where she needed to be.

Okay, she wouldn't walk off that Memphis train into the able hands of her Novo Mundum contact as planned. But if she could get closer to the community, which, from Ineo's clues, she guessed to be somewhere in the Midwest, Keely felt sure she would find a guide to lead her safely to Novo Mundum.

Keeping her eyes on the pavement, she thought of Ineo. She'd looked peaceful. Rested. Happy, even. Ineo understood what the world had come to, and the secret to her happiness lay in the knowledge that she was part of something better. Something more hopeful. A place where the world would be new again.

Catching movement out of the corner of her eye, Keely turned quickly, but no one was there. Was someone shadowing her? Or was it just nerves?

As she crossed St. Peter Street, a pair of kids wandered out of the junglelike remains of a park to her left and headed her way. The boy was her age or maybe a little older, dressed in loose jeans and a white tank; the girl was younger, her black hair pinned on top of her head, three sprays of crimped waves sticking out like plumes.

"Hey, there," the boy said, his accent loose and warm. The couple stopped in front of her, blocking her way.

"Hey." Keely had started to move around them when the girl leaned into her.

"You're not from around here, huh?" The girl's mellow drawl held the hint of a threat. The beaded earrings dangling almost to her T-shirt caught the late-morning sunlight as she moved.

Keely's heart raced. They were just kids, like her, but there was an edge in their eyes. A hunger.

"I'm just passing through," Keely said. "Excuse me."

"What's your hurry?" The boy sidled closer and slung his arm around Keely's shoulders. She felt his fingers dangling near the strap to her backpack. Oh God, was he going to rob her?

"No hurry. Just got somewhere I need to be," Keely said, faking a boldness she didn't feel.

"That's not very polite, is it, Kev?" the girl said, reaching out to touch Keely's hair. "I like that pack. Used to have one just like it, you know? I'd be happy to carry it for you, and Kev'll show you around the neighborhood."

"Tour guides, huh?" a voice behind Keely said, and she whirled around to see Amber, the girl from the train station, rooted to the sidewalk, hands curled into fists. How the hell did she get here?

"We know where we're going," Amber said pointedly. "Thanks, anyway. But there's a couple of choice-looking senior citizens back about two blocks. Why don't you knock them over? Ten points if you make the old lady cry."

"Ain't you sweet?" the boy said, letting his arm drop from Keely's shoulders and swiveling around to check out Amber.

"Actually, no," Amber said. "Not sweet at all."

That was the point at which Keely noticed the gleaming blade of an army knife protruding from Amber's right fist. Amber hefted it casually. Then, reaching out, she sliced a loose thread off Kev's shirt. The blade flashed in the sun. Keely watched in awe as Kev and the strange girl shrank back.

"No harm done," Kev said, raising his hands. "We were just being neighborly."

"Find a new neighborhood, then," Amber said, and Keely felt a startled grin spread over her face as the pair walked away.

Amber flicked the blade shut. "Bad Keely. Just can't keep out of trouble, can you?"

Keely sagged as relief set in. "I guess not."

NINETEEN

MICHAEL WINCED AT THE STAB OF PAIN AND LIFTED A BLIS-
tered hand from the oar. One of the bubbles had
popped, and the skin was red and raw and grey with
grime.

"What's wrong?" Maggie asked from her hunched
position in the bow of the canoe. She'd learned to nap
that way, which was fine with Michael since he'd rather
have her tune out than whine the whole time he paddled them down the Ohio River.

"Nothing," Michael muttered.

"Whatever." Maggie shook her head and gazed
across the water.

For one moment Michael flashed back to the early
days of their relationship. The times when it seemed

like they couldn't stop talking, touching, dreaming together. When the sound of her laugh or her voice could make his day lift. But now . . . Now just her presence set his teeth on edge.

They'd been paddling for days, stopping occasionally to search abandoned riverside homes for dry clothes, food, and water. Since their brush with the cops in Cincinnati they'd covered miles of mostly deserted land, trying to avoid the alleys of death untouched by any Decontamination Unit. There'd been a quick confrontation with two old ladies who'd obviously evaded the army roundups. They lived in an abandoned-looking old house on a hill overlooking the river. Maggie had tried to make nice with them, but when the shotguns came out, even she had realized it was best to stay in the canoe and move on. There were signs of life here and there, evidence that someone was still around somewhere or maybe soldiers patrolling.

Otherwise the Big Empty was . . . empty. Empty cupboards, empty homes, empty roads, if you didn't count the occasional pockets of uncollected corpses, turned now to sun-bleached skeletons. Michael shivered, remembering a trailer park littered with bones.

It was eerie poking around in the debris of strangers' lives, but scavenging was their only means of survival. Both Michael and Maggie had traded in their shoes for work boots they'd found at an old shoe repair shop. They'd found flannel shirts, down vests, bristly blankets, and cans of potatoes and beans and fruit cocktail, along with a few decorative canisters of dried pasta that cooked up okay. Every time Maggie complained, Michael reminded her that the stakes had changed. This was twofold survival, scraping together enough resources to stay alive while running from the law.

Maggie was pressing to head south, to some city out of the Evacuated Zones, but Michael didn't think that was a good idea. He had no idea how the new government worked with criminals, what kinds of systems they had to track people down. But what if there was information on Maggie and him going around to police in all the remaining cities? Besides, Maggie had an astonishing knack for getting into trouble; it was as if she were hardwired for it. No, a city didn't make sense. But if not a city, where?

Michael flexed his aching palms and laid the oars across his knees, giving himself a break. "Listen, we've got to make a choice up here," he said. "Looks like we're about to hit the fork of the Mississippi and Ohio rivers, and I think it's time we ditch the canoe and find a place to hole up for a while."

"My feet are so cold," Maggie said, shifting on her seat. "These boots would be warm if they would stay dry. How come you picked a canoe with a hole in it?"

"Just lucky, I guess."

"We need to switch directions, go someplace warmer," Maggie declared. "Wouldn't it be nice to go to Florida?" Her eyes grew soft, far away. "You know, find a beach and just hang. I could really toast my toes in some warm sand. That would be a riot, right? Live off oranges like natives and kick back until we figure out what to do?"

Michael bit the insides of his cheeks to keep from lashing out at her. Didn't she know that orange trees didn't actually grow right on the beach? And staying warm might be easy in Florida, but what about staying dry? And what natives was she talking about, anyway? She was so unrealistic. And he was sick of taking care of everything while she fantasized about catching a savage tan on the beach.

"Hey, paddle boy," she teased, her voice sexy and syrupy. "Let's turn this thing around and head down to the Florida Keys?"

"Just shut up, okay?"

She looked startled, as if he'd slapped her, then quickly recovered. She grinned. "Whoa. Somebody woke up on the wrong side of the canoe."

"That would imply I got some sleep, which I didn't," Michael said.

"Is that why you're so cranky?" Her full lips turned down in a pout. "I just can't do anything right by you, can I, Michael? I mean, what do you want from me?"

"I want you to use your head," he snapped. "I want you to think before you dive into the next catastrophe."

Maggie's eyes went wide. "Why are you being so mean?"

"So you can get the big picture!" He heard his voice rising. "There's no going back to the populated areas, Maggie! Take a look at those maps we swiped and get to know the Big Empty, because it's going to be your home for a long time."

She stared back at him, her eyes tearing up.

"Oh, Michael," she whispered, her eyes never leaving his face. "This is really happening. It's not ever going to be okay again, is it?"

Michael's chest felt tight. He didn't know what to say to her. To himself. His jaw clenched hard, his breath shortened, and he fought back tears of his own.

Maggie lunged at him from the bow, sloshing water into the canoe.

"Watch it!" Michael yelped, clutching the oars so they wouldn't fall out of the boat. Maggie knelt in front of him, her arms around him, and buried her face against his shoulder. Michael shut his eyes and let himself feel her warmth against him. He slid the oars onto the floor of the boat and embraced Maggie.

"I'm sorry," she murmured over and over into his down vest.

Hearing her finally say those words made his hardness toward her melt a tiny bit, created a small enough crack in his armored stance to let her slip back in.

"You didn't do anything on purpose," he whispered hoarsely. He fought back tears, fear, and desire for this girl he no longer even liked. But for this one minute, her soft lips now on his cheek, his neck, and then his lips, Maggie was how he could bear the silent, death-filled expanse of the Big Empty. If only for a little while. So he would let her win him over again the way she used to. Before everything had changed.

TWENTY

NIGHT HAD FALLEN OVER NEW ORLEANS WHEN AMBER TWISTED around on the park bench, checking the security guard in his booth near the imposing wrought-iron gate to the freight yard.

"I can't believe I'm doing this," Keely said.

"Don't worry," Amber said. "These places put on skeleton crews at night. I'll take care of the guard, you do your part, and in a few minutes we'll be headed north on the Polar Express."

Keely shook her head, but she backed away from the gate as instructed. "Here goes." She huddled in a doorway a few yards away.

Amber stepped up to the heavy gate and gave it a shake. "Sir!" she called, making her voice as young and helpless as possible. "Sir, can you help me?"

The guard ambled over, hands in his pockets, frowning. "Yeah?"

Amber's bottom lip trembled as she made up a story about a little brother with his foot caught in a sewer grate two blocks away. "He's just five, sir, and he's so scared! Can you please help me get him out? You gotta help us!"

"I can't leave the premises," the guard said. "But you can go to the police station."

"I don't know where that is! We're new here." She was crying in earnest now, tears sliding down her cheeks. *I should really be an actress. If they ever start making movies again.*

The man was softening like butter in the sun. "Miss, I'm not supposed to leave my post. The police station is that way, though. They'll help you." He pointed down the street.

Man, I hadn't expected him to put up such a fight. He didn't seem like someone who'd been a security guard pre–Strain 7—he looked more like the type who'd ended up with the job when whatever he used to do became pointless. Maybe that was why he was extra nervous about cutting her a break, though.

She pressed her face into the fence, pleading. "Can you show me? I'm not sure which block you mean. Around the park or through it?"

The man looked around and then sighed. "Okay, but it has to be quick," he said, fumbling with the lock. As he stepped onto the sidewalk, she tugged his hand before he could close the gate behind him.

"Hurry, please!" she begged.

If Keely was doing her part, she was creeping in behind them, heading for the office beyond the security guard's booth.

Give her a minute to check the schedules and find the right track, Amber thought. She nodded at the man, pretending to listen to his instructions. *Okay, that's long enough.*

Time to change tactics.

"Can't you call the police?" she pleaded. "Or let me use the phone? It would be quicker, right? Please, sir, I can't let anything happen to him. He's my only brother now. He's all I have left."

"Well . . ." Wavering, the man nodded and turned back to the gate. "There's a phone in the booth. Come on."

"Oh, thank you," she gushed. She followed him in, dramatically wiping tears from her cheeks. Inside the booth she pretended to make her call, then thanked him again.

"I'll let myself out," she said, hoisting her heavy backpack. "Gotta get back to little Carter. And I wouldn't want to get you in any trouble."

"Good luck, kid," the security guard called with a fatherly nod over his clipboard.

Amber backed out of the booth, waiting until the guard wasn't looking, and then swerved out to the train yard. She cut around the first engine till she was out of view, then raced between tracks, looking for Keely.

She was beginning to have fun with this.

She'd been ready to change course when Carter blew her off, but since then she'd gotten her second wind. Amber was going to Novo Mundum. The morning's confrontation with Carter was far from over. Now more than ever she was itching to blast him, particularly in front of the do-gooders at this secret place. They needed to know what a major jerk he was. That was Amber's new personal mission. In fact, once those people heard the truth, they'd probably be welcoming Amber in and throwing Carter out on his butt.

The tracks curved to the right, and at last she saw Keely ahead, waving a tiny penlight.

The train to St. Louis was humming with the vibration of the warming engine. They walked down the line of cars, past cylinders of propane, a freezer car that reeked of fish, containers of grain. At last they found a container with foam mattresses covered in clear plastic. Amber pushed her backpack inside, then swung herself onto the metal grate behind Keely, who lugged their backpacks away from the door.

"What the hell do you have in here? Gold bricks?" Keely asked, sagging under the weight of Amber's backpack.

"Better. A laptop." Amber brushed off her hands.

"Are you kidding me?" Keely gasped. "As soon as we get off this train and find a working phone jack, we can send a message to Novo Mundum. They can notify my guide to meet us in St. Louis instead." Keely shook her head. "I can't believe you have a computer. Does it work okay?"

"I don't like to waste the battery, but yeah, we can send a short message," Amber said. She tested a pile of mattresses. "How long is this trip going to take?"

Keely planted herself cross-legged in the center of one mattress. "I checked the old schedule, and the passenger trains to St. Louis used to take between sixteen and nineteen hours." She rubbed her eyes. "Man, I'm wiped out."

Amber leaned back and flailed her arms and legs, as if she could make a snow angel on the mattress. For the first time in weeks she actually felt like smiling. "Well, all you have to do right now is kick back and enjoy the ride."

TWENTY-ONE

THE SUN WAS HOT ON JONAH DALTON'S BACK AS HE REELED IN his line. Aw, man . . . he'd felt a tug, but some fish had gone and stolen the last of his bait.

Oh, well. Might as well head in since it was getting hot on the lake. At home in Atlanta he'd never questioned the fact that summer lasted well into October, but he was surprised to find it so warm up here in Missouri. Sunlight glinted off the surface of the lake like strings of diamonds, and he carefully placed the rowboat's oars into the metal channels that held them out of the water while he stripped off his jacket.

Four fat, silvery fish wriggled in a bucket at his feet. He had no idea what they were, but he knew they'd be delicious. Maybe more so because he'd caught them himself, he thought, taking up the oars and slowly turning the boat toward the house where he'd been staying for the past two weeks.

Rowing toward the house, Jonah wondered if his guide would show today to take him the rest of the way to Novo Mundum. He'd been restless and bored for days. Mickey and Atom, the middle-aged couple who ran the way station, were nice and all, but he hadn't come all the way from Atlanta to laze around some abandoned lake house reading old paperbacks and trying to count the stars each night.

Every evening at supper Mickey reassured him that the guide would make it through soon. "It's just that things are getting tighter here, with the renegades and the army patrolling," she'd told him last night, playing with the end of her thick black braid. "I'm sure that's the reason for the delay. Remember, above all, we have to protect the community at Novo Mundum. We're all taking a lesson from what happened at Green Forge."

Jonah had heard about that. The government broadcast station had blared reports about an "anti-American" community in the heart of Kansas that had been raided, where soldiers had "successfully quelled the dangerous rebellion." In other words, they'd killed nearly a hundred residents before the siege ended. The way the news made it sound, the residents of Green Forge were about to launch nuclear war on the rest of the country. Jonah had bought into those stories too until he met Mickey and Atom and heard the other side of things. According to them, the only crime those people had committed was that they'd existed in an E Zone in Kansas and hadn't wanted to evacuate and live under all the new, heavy-duty rules and regulations of MacCauley and his board.

Mickey was right—the guide was probably just being cautious—but that didn't make it any easier to wait. It was hard to understand how she and Atom could live out here alone, fishing for their dinner and growing vegetables in the small garden Mickey had planted. They acted like they'd landed in some rural paradise and seemed content to drift along day to day with no one but each other for company and the occasional recruit passing through.

It was just plain weird.

But *they* weren't weird, he thought with a stab of guilt. They were happy, and that was the point. It was why he'd come all this way, wasn't it? To escape grim Atlanta, the shattered city where he'd grown up, where he'd been alone even before Strain 7 had killed his parents.

He rowed harder, feeling the muscles in his arms warming with the exercise. It had been a long time since he'd triggered the old guilt—guilt over the fact that he'd felt little when his parents died. Just a numbness that gave way to relief that he would never again have to listen to them shouting at each other, never have to endure his father's beatings or his mother's rages, never again have to disappear into the garage with the excuse of needing the hammer.

A lot of resentment and frustration could be pounded away with nothing more than a basic set of Craftsman tools. He was sometimes tempted to use them to smash the broken TV or the ugly elephant-shaped vase his mother's aunt had sent one Christmas, but somehow he always managed to restrain himself.

Jonah flinched as a bird shot out of the trees and swooped low, skimming the surface of the water. "You are such a city boy," he said, chuckling softly.

If he could just learn to relax, spending time out here would probably seem like a vacation. Once you got used to all the nature sounds, the birds and insects and frogs, it was actually pretty sweet to forget about the virus, the devastation, all the grim, sour people left behind. Out there he'd passed lines of displaced people heading south to escape the cold weather or the army or to simply keep moving away from the past, putting distance between themselves and the ruins of their lives. Out there people smashed windows to steal food and medical supplies. Out there people traded batteries for boxes of stale crackers. Kids sucked ketchup out of wrinkled takeout packets from trashed fast-food restaurants.

But here it was almost possible to believe none of that existed. That life could have a rhythm and sense to it.

He shielded his eyes from the glare on the water and gazed toward shore. Their dock was one of more than a dozen spread along that shore of the lake, but it was easy to spot the house—big, white, and old-fashioned, with faded green shutters.

And a red bucket hanging over the back porch rail.

He pulled the oars out of the water, a shiver of alarm racing down his back. That was the warning signal, a sign something was wrong. Mickey had given him the drill the first day he'd arrived. If he was ever away from the house, she'd said, and returned to see that red bucket, he was supposed to run the other way and head west, to a town called Clearwater.

So much for paradise.

He ducked halfway down in the boat and took the oars again. What was he supposed to do now? Running away—abandoning Mickey and Atom if they were in trouble—seemed so wrong.

But Mickey had been so clear. Go. Go and keep going on to Clearwater.

Screw that. He had to help them. Maybe if he startled whoever had shown up, he could save Mickey and Atom. Maybe they didn't even need saving. Maybe the bucket was just a precaution because they'd heard a weird noise or seen something in the bushes. Maybe—

He noticed movement—a man, but it wasn't Atom. Not unless he'd shaved his head into a buzz cut in the hours Jonah had been gone. And started carrying a rifle.

Dropping the oars on the floor, Jonah dove down with them, his heart banging as he breathed in the pungent stink of the fish. He could feel the boat drifting. God, he hoped it was heading away from the dock.

A man with a gun meant real trouble. Nothing he'd be able to help with. As much as he hated to leave Mickey and Atom, he had to get the hell away from there. By himself.

TWENTY-TWO

IRENE CROUCHED IN THE CORNER OF THE LITTLE APARTMENT IN Clearwater, her eyes never leaving Diego on the bed across the small room. He had started bleeding again— lightly this time, thank goodness—but a body just can't keep on losing blood.

She wrapped her arms around her knees and hugged herself tight. *This is my fault,* kept running through her head. *I should never have moved him, not with a bullet wound. That's like, rule number one, isn't it? But I didn't really have a choice,* she assured herself. And besides, Diego had insisted, even teasing that he would hold the gun on her if she refused. Fat chance, since he couldn't have gotten up to get it.

Her heart expanded in her chest, reaching out toward

him. His courage was inspirational. Diego had endured the bumpy ride, his leg propped up by a bag of rice and jars of peaches cushioned by an old comforter, as Irene pulled the wagon. Not only had he endured, he had encouraged her, kept her going by telling her stories, mostly about life with his Nonnie. She sounded like a tough old lady, that Nonnie, and Irene figured that Diego had inherited a lot of his grit from her. Together they had navigated the roads to Clearwater, where they'd moved into this small apartment behind the post office.

The trip here had nearly killed him—nearly killed her too, come to think of it—and Irene wasn't even sure if Clearwater was their real destination. She had no idea where Novo Mundum really was. There had been no explicit instructions other than "north" and a hunch.

Diego moaned and moved on the bed, making Irene's heart clutch. *He can't die, he just can't.* That would be too much to bear; she was responsible for him. She wouldn't be able to cope if she were to lose Diego now, not after losing so much else.

When she saw the first sign for Clearwater, she'd almost shouted with relief. But then reality set in. Clearwater was just another abandoned town. Prettier than most, with its lakeside setting, charming bed-and-breakfasts, and old-fashioned main street with little apartments above or behind the storefronts, but still, it was empty. And had been for a long time. It obviously wasn't Novo Mundum, and Irene had no idea how to get them there—and Novo Mundum was Diego's only hope.

And worst of all had been *her own* hope. She had

believed, secretly, deep down in her heart of hearts, that they'd come here and find her father and her brother, Aaron, hiding out. "The guide wouldn't let us go back," her dad would have explained. "We had to follow the rules."

"You must have passed the guide on your way here and not realized," Aaron would have added. They would have had a good long laugh about it—and hugs, and tears, and whatever it was that they used to do.

"You should wheel me to the woods," Diego said softly from the bed, interrupting her imaginary conversation.

Irene jumped up. She had thought he was asleep. "What?" she asked, crossing quickly to the bed. She sat on the edge, hiding her concern when she saw that there was fresh blood on the sheets.

I wonder if that antibiotic stops blood from clotting. Soon after they'd arrived in Clearwater, she'd found some antibiotic powder in the pharmacy, which she'd mixed with water to give Diego. But she wasn't sure of the dose or the medicine's strength or contraindications.

"Hunting doesn't require feet, now that I've got customized wheels," Diego said, pointing to the wheelchair they'd also found in the back of the pharmacy. "You can wheel me out into the woods, let me sit till I've got a good shot. I'll even use my longbow if the rifle bothers you."

"That's sporting of you," Irene said as she checked the gauze she'd wrapped around Diego's leg. "But the hunting can wait."

"We need food, don't we? Aren't you hungry?"

"I'm fine," she lied.

"Okay, then, just order us a pizza. Deep dish, extra cheese." He closed his eyes, then added, "Pepperoni."

Irene swallowed hard, trying not to think about the mouthwatering image. "I'll call in the order," she said as his breathing began to slow down and deepen.

Diego was asleep again, which was an almost constant thing in the past two days.

Well, lose that much blood, you're going to feel weak, she figured.

She crept out of the bedroom, quietly made her way out of the apartment, and sprinted down the street in the cool open air. The sidewalk was wet from the rain the night before. The blacktop at the service station glistened with rainbows, the rain smearing the last remnants of spilled oil on the pavement's surface. She jogged down Main Street toward Eighth, heading for the service station on the corner. If she was lucky, she'd find a map of Clearwater there, even if it was only one of the hand-drawn, cartoonish ones intended for tourists. She had to figure out a way to Novo Mundum.

It was an old-fashioned station, although peering inside, she guessed that they'd once stocked basic groceries, doughnuts, and coffee. Too bad all the shelves were empty now.

When she pushed open the door to the office, the bell jangled, startling her. Every noise was too loud in the silence out here. No matter how barren the place seemed, you couldn't take chances. She and her dad and Aaron had thought they were alone up until the moment she'd discovered Diego, shot by the soldier, so close to their campsite. Who knew when someone else might come through this town, checking to make sure everyone had left like they were supposed to?

Inside the station she couldn't stop imagining the people who used to occupy this town, pumping gas, delivering mail, chowing down on BLTs at Dinah's Luncheonette. Although she knew some were dead and others had evacuated, their ghosts lingered, complaining about the price of coffee, remarking about the change in weather, bragging about a win in the bowling tournament. Having lives.

Irene shook off her sense of ghosts and slid behind the counter, noticing the thick white dust that coated everything. A revolving wire rack of maps and postcards was set up beside the counter, and she spun it, wincing at the angry whine of the un-oiled metal.

She found a tourist brochure of lakes of the Ozarks. That might help, but she wanted something more specific. She was refolding the brochure when a movement outside the window caught her eye.

An animal? she thought, her heart hammering. *Please be an animal.*

She ducked behind a vending machine, her heart racing as a rattling noise echoed in the street.

People. But who? Residents of Clearwater who'd disobeyed the law and stuck around, like Diego at his farm? Her contact from Novo Mundum?

Or maybe more soldiers, like the one who shot Diego.

TWENTY-THREE

KEELY CLENCHED HER TEETH AS AMBER KICKED THE CAN again, sending it skittering across the street. "Would you cut it out?" Keely snapped, "We don't want to attract attention, remember?" She lowered her backpack to an abandoned trailer hitch in the junk heap next to the gas station. A pebble had been rolling around in her shoe for a while, and she perched on the bed of the hitch, wishing for clean socks as she yanked off her boot.

"Besides, shouldn't you sit down, rest? I mean, considering?"

Amber narrowed her eyes at her. "What's that supposed to mean?"

Keely paused. She'd been debating whether to admit

what she knew from the moment she began to put the clues together—something about Amber's appearance and how she kept getting sick in the early parts of the day. Then there'd been the time when Amber hadn't realized Keely was watching her, and she'd had her hand on her stomach with a concerned, overwhelmed expression in her eyes.

"So what, you know?" Amber asked when Keely didn't say anything.

Keely bit her lip, then nodded. "It's all the more reason why we need to get to Novo Mundum," she said. "So you can *both* be safe."

"Well, if you haven't noticed, Clearwater is a bust," Amber said, hands on her hips. "I think you screwed up when you decoded that last message."

"I got it right," Keely told Amber. "You saw me decode it."

Amber folded her arms. "So why are we not in the Magic Kingdom yet?"

"Were you expecting a parade? Novo Mundum can't be that obvious. It's not a place you just walk into, not out here in the Big Empty." She tugged her shoe back on and laced it up. "They're probably sending a guide to meet us here. We'll e-mail them again, tell them we're here and waiting for further instruction."

Amber peeled off her packs and sat down beside Keely. "I don't know why they have to be so secretive. It's not like we've seen anyone out here."

"Because we've been careful," Keely said. She frowned. "Until you started kicking cans around. There *are* people out here, Amber. Don't be fooled by the silence."

As if on cue, a scrape of metal sent Keely's pulse racing. Her head twitched up to the source of the noise—a girl standing in the doorway of the gas station.

A teenage girl with short dark, curls. Keely felt her shoulders sag in relief. This girl wasn't a soldier. And she didn't look like one of those scary renegades, either. She looked like a normal girl, like . . .

Maybe a guide?

Quickly Keely lifted her fingertips to her chin in greeting. "I've been searching for my father, Albert Camus," she said, quoting the code phrase that Ineo had taught her.

The girl shook her head, looking disappointed. "Sorry. I'm looking for him too."

"This is all very 007 of you both," Amber said, rolling her eyes, "but maybe we can cut to the chase?" She eyed the strange girl. "Are you looking for Novo Mundum?"

Keely bristled, hearing Amber mention the secret community to the stranger, but judging from her response to Keely's greeting, she figured the girl was okay.

Raking the curls out of her eyes, the other girl answered, "Well, yeah."

Keely's heart sank. "So you're not our guide?" she asked.

"I wish," the other girl said. "My name is Irene, and I'm a seeker too."

"Oh." Keely sat back on the trailer. Disappointment rushed through her, and she suddenly felt all of her exhaustion.

"I'm here with my friend Diego," Irene continued. "We've been holed up here for, I don't know, nearly six days now."

"Nothing personal, Irene," Amber said. "But what the hell have you been doing all this time? I mean, just sitting on your butts in this dump for days?" She shook her head and scowled. "Aren't you guys beginning to wonder if these Novo Mundum freaks are yanking your chain?"

Irene blinked, obviously not sure what to make of Amber.

"Amber's got trust issues," Keely intervened. "But I think we've got a lot to talk about, Irene. Let's get off the street, okay?"

Irene nodded. "Come back to our place. We've even got a stove that works on propane." She smiled sheepishly. "Which would be really great if we had some food."

"Hey, hot water works for me." Amber's eyes sparkled with new energy as she grabbed her backpacks. "I knew those tea bags would come in handy."

"And we can boil our socks," Keely blurted. When Amber wrinkled her nose, Keely laughed. "I never thought I'd miss laundry day, but right now it seems like a luxury to boil my underwear."

TWENTY-FOUR

JONAH TOOK THE DENTED PAN OFF THE CAMPFIRE AND SET IT on a rock. The fish smelled good, but he wasn't hungry. Every time he thought of what had happened at Atom and Mickey's place, his stomach turned over in a sickening roll—and he'd thought about it pretty much non-stop since the scene at the lake house three days ago.

He'd stayed low in the drifting boat until it had bumped against something hard. He'd landed at a dock three down from the house. Taking a chance, he'd slipped the rope over the peg on the dock and climbed out, the pail and his fishing rod banging against his thigh as he ran for the trees.

After assuring himself that no one had noticed him, he'd snuck closer to Mickey and Atom's place, going from tree to tree. He had to find out what was going on. He'd just taken cover behind a hydrangea bush when he heard a noise. When he got his breathing enough under control that he could peek out from his hiding place, he was surprised by the sight of an old-fashioned cart drawn by a horse. One man controlled the horse; the other was pushing Atom and Mickey into the back of the cart. Jonah's chest tightened when he saw that his friends were bound and gagged. He stared at the strange men and noticed that each sported a gash across his right cheek.

The Slash.

Mickey had told him about the renegades when she explained the red bucket signal. They were off-gridders, rebels—violent ones. Each member of the gang submitted to the mark on his cheek as a sign of solidarity. Mickey and Atom had heard that any hostages they took were slashed the same way. No one knew where their headquarters was, but lately the mostly male renegades had been scouring this part of the Big Empty, scavenging for food, fuel, supplies, and women.

It all suddenly fell into place for Jonah. He had been so naive. The Slash's presence in this area explained why his guide hadn't shown up as scheduled. Mickey had only hinted; she had never explicitly said that she was afraid the Slash had taken his guide out. But now, seeing them, Jonah realized that was obviously the reason.

After he was sure the Slash had left, Jonah had spent that night at the house, huddled in the dark with a baseball bat he'd found in the shed, hoping that Mickey and Atom had escaped and were on their way back. But as the grandfather clock in the living room ticked off each hour, he knew they hadn't been that lucky. And since the men had taken most of the supplies in the house—including Jonah's backpack, which contained all his clothes and his worn copy of *The Chocolate War*—his only choice was to head to Clearwater, following Mickey's instructions.

All by himself. That was the worst part—being alone again. It was the prime reason he'd decided to join Novo Mundum—to be part of a working team. A family. The family he'd never had. Well, once he got to Novo Mundum, everything would change.

If he got there.

A wet splash from the lake made the tiny hairs on the back of Jonah's neck prickle. He heard a girl's voice. Mickey? The voice sounded younger than Mickey's, and he was miles from the way station, but it didn't stop him from hoping.

Scrambling up, he made his way through the trees until the lake came into view. A girl his age stood shivering on a rock, her drenched clothes pasted to her thin frame. She laughed as she shook droplets of water from her hair.

Well, she wasn't with the Slash, at least—but she also didn't seem too concerned about keeping a low profile. Maybe she was one of their girls? Jonah crept softly through the underbrush.

"Hey!" she called, spotting him. She acted like they

were meeting at a summer resort, friendly strangers swimming off the dock. Was that a good sign or a bad sign? he wondered.

"Hey," he called back, stepping out from behind a tree cautiously. She had to be part of Novo Mundum. Otherwise why was she here? Of course she was. Which reminded him . . . the code. "Hey, I'm looking for my father—" he began.

A sharp probe between his shoulder blades cut off the rest of Jonah's words.

"Hands in the air," said a low voice.

Crap.

TWENTY-FIVE

"I'M COOL," THE GUY SAID, HOLDING UP HIS HANDS. "DON'T hurt me."

Leave Maggie alone for one minute and what does she do? Michael fumed. *She starts talking to strangers. Does that girl have any sense at all?*

He was disappointed in her but more disappointed in himself for thinking that maybe, just maybe, she'd really take in what was happening and start behaving responsibly for a change.

No such luck.

"We really hope you're not a cop," Maggie said. She made an exaggerated grimace. "We don't like cops." Then she gave the guy a winning grin.

"Do I look like law enforcement to you?" the guy asked.

Michael lowered the stick and stepped around for a better look. "Who are you?" he demanded.

As the stranger caught sight of Michael's makeshift weapon, a rueful smile spread over his face. "Nice trick."

That was when Michael realized the guy was just a kid—a teenager with haunted eyes and smooth, dark skin. His broad shoulders and solid, muscular build had made him look older at first.

"My name's Jonah," he said. He eyed Maggie and Michael curiously. "Who are you? Nobody's supposed to be way out here."

"We know that," Maggie admitted. "I'm Maggie, and he's Michael." She clasped her hands together and gasped dramatically. "Oh no, he knows our names. Now we'll have to kill him."

Michael winced. Those kinds of jokes were just not funny. Not anymore.

The stranger moved a few feet away from Michael. He glanced back and forth between Maggie, still in the water, and Michael, a few feet away.

Michael noticed that Maggie's wet clothing was practically see-through and plastered against her body. Jonah seemed more uncomfortable about it than Maggie did. His dark eyes kept flicking away from her.

"You guys on your way somewhere?" Jonah asked.

"Just camping," Michael said, keeping his tone flat. Maggie might like taking chances, but he didn't. "Enjoying the great outdoors."

Jonah's eyebrows rose in disbelief. "Camping in the Big Empty?"

"It's a long story," Michael said. "How about you? Did you say you were looking for someone? Your father?"

Jonah tucked his hands into the back pockets of his jeans, leaning back to assess Michael. "I've got a long story too. But I've also got some fish fried if you're hungry." He shrugged. "I can't eat them all."

"Fish?" Maggie gaped at him. "Not out of a can, you mean?"

"The real thing." Jonah flashed a grin, revealing even white teeth. "Just through the woods there."

Maggie charged out of the water. "Come on, Michael. I know you're ravenous."

That was the truth. And the thought of real food—fresh fish cooked over a fire—made his stomach rumble in anticipation. It wouldn't hurt to share Jonah's meal, since he was offering. It also wouldn't hurt to hear his story. Maybe he had information that could help them.

They arrived at Jonah's campsite. God, it smelled good. Michael sat down on a weathered log and was surprised when Jonah reached into his pocket and pulled out an army knife. "Here," he told Michael casually. "You can use it to eat if you want."

Handing him a knife? Jonah was generous *and* trusting. Michael relaxed, just a notch. He opened the knife and chose a thin blade for spearing the fish. "Nice knife," he admitted. It sported two screwdrivers, scissors, and a pair of pliers among nearly two dozen other tools. "You find it out here?"

Jonah shook his head. "It belonged to someone close to me. You know, who died."

"Your dad?" Maggie said, wiping her mouth with the back of her hand.

"No." Jonah's dark eyes darkened more. "It was my shop teacher's, actually. He was a good guy."

Feelings obviously flooded into Jonah; it made Michael look away.

"This is so delish. Where are you from, Jonah?" Maggie asked.

"Atlanta." Jonah speared the last of the fish and held it out to Maggie. "I'm on my way to a town called Clearwater, west of here. To, uh . . . meet some friends."

Friends? Out here? Michael frowned.

But Maggie seemed interested. "Really?" she asked. She flashed him one of her most disarming smiles and let the blanket drop off her shoulders. With her T-shirt still wet, Jonah was getting a full view of her shapely breasts.

Jonah swiveled to face Michael. "You can come if you want," he said. "I mean, if you're not headed somewhere else."

"How far is it?" Michael asked.

"And how are you getting there?" Maggie chimed in. "I am so sick of canoes."

"Oh, it's not too far," Jonah said quickly. "I was planning to use a bike I found up at one of the houses. I bet we could find a couple more."

Michael finished the last of his fish and carefully wiped the knife's blade on the edge of his T-shirt before handing it back to Jonah. Why was this kid so eager for them to join him? It was setting off alarms in Michael's head. Then again, even if he didn't completely trust Jonah, what were his other options? They had to keep moving. Might as well travel with someone who could at least earn his keep along the way. Besides, Jonah's presence might make it easier to deal with Maggie.

Ever since they had hooked up again in the canoe, Michael's guilt had grown. How could he have done that? He knew he didn't want to be with her anymore; he had taken advantage of her. Unfortunately, it had also made Maggie behave as if she could do no wrong with him—whining, complaining, and continuing to take stupid risks. He wasn't sure how much more he could take.

"I'm with you, Jonah," Maggie said. She gave Michael a challenging look. "That's my vote. On bikes. How about you, Mikey?"

Michael ignored her patronizing tone and wondered if maybe she was hot for Jonah. That would suit him just fine. He wasn't just going to send her on her own with a stranger, though. And maybe Clearwater would be a decent place to stay while he figured out his next move.

"Okay," Michael said, glancing at Jonah. "Count us in."

TWENTY-SIX

THE PERFECT SHOT.

Somehow Diego knew that if he waited long enough here at the edge of the trail, it would come to him. It had better, since this wheelchair wouldn't go much farther in the damp leaves and moss off the trail.

Irene was going to be mad. She was always warning him to take it easy. Stay in bed. Swallow the drugs and sleep. But he was sick of being the burden, the deadweight to be lugged around. And with two new girls here and nothing to eat but rice and peaches, he couldn't lie around like a loaf. One shot with his longbow and they could all fill up on wild turkey.

The sounds of the woods closed in around him, swarming insects and fluttering birds. He shifted in the chair, wondering if he could sleep here with his eyelids open. He felt so weary and bloodless, fragile and worn. But maybe he could use that lack of energy to calmly woo his prey. A Zen turkey shoot.

Hell, the birds were so stupid, he could probably spin wheelies in the chair and not scare them off.

He might have dozed, or maybe he just blinked for a moment, but his eyes were closed when he heard the cackle of a wild bird. He pulled a bow from the quiver and lined it up. *Keep the shooting eye open. Look for the tail feathers. Aim for the heart.*

He might be lame, but he'd be damned if he couldn't survive on this land, his Missouri. Holding his breath, he let the arrow fly.

TWENTY-SEVEN

"THAT DINNER KNOCKED ME OUT," KEELY SAID WITH A YAWN. They had just eaten an unbelievable meal of baked apples and turkey stuffed with rice.

"It's the tryptophan in the turkey," Irene said. "Irresistible. Diego and Amber have already succumbed." She stacked the last dish beside the sink and came over to the couch, where Keely sat in front of the open computer. "How's it going?"

Curled up under a blanket, Keely had been working on a message to send to Novo Mundum, telling them she was waiting in Clearwater for a guide. "I'm just double-checking my message, making sure I've got the numeric cipher right."

Irene nodded. "Good thing we've got you. If I got an

e-mail of numbers or jumbled letters, I wouldn't know how to begin deciphering them. Novo Mundum always contacted my dad."

"I've always liked puzzles," Keely said as she clicked send. She shut the computer and leaned back into the sofa. "I wonder how long it'll take a guide to get here?"

"I hope it's soon," Irene said quietly. "Diego needs real medical attention. I don't think he's going to heal until that bullet comes out."

"We'll get there," Keely promised.

Irene held her gaze for a second, and Keely could see just how scared she really was.

"Oh . . . I almost forgot," Irene said, jumping up, breaking the moment. "I've got a present for you." She reached behind her, then turned and held up a pair of fluffy white women's socks. "I thought you could use these while your socks are drying out."

"They look brand-new!" Keely pressed them to her cheek, then quickly slid them on. Knees to her chin, she rubbed the smooth cotton over her feet.

New socks.

For some stupid reason Keely suddenly felt like she was about to cry. It was so nice of Irene to do that for her. It hit her that she hadn't been around that kind of thoughtfulness for a long time. Not since Bree had given her the pendant, begging Keely not to give up on life even though so many lives were gone.

"Thanks," Keely said, blinking a couple of times. "Where did you get them?"

"The apartment upstairs. Must have been a woman there. Left everything behind."

Keely nodded. The woman must have not had anyone to cart away her stuff. She forced her thoughts about the woman dying alone up there aside.

Irene leaned back against the sofa. "So . . . who did you lose?" she asked.

Keely flinched, remembering when that used to be such a common question. Even all this time later it was always in the air whenever you met someone new. "My father. A boyfriend," she said. "My little sister, Bree."

"I'm sorry," Irene said softly. "You know . . . when my mother died, it nearly destroyed my father. The trip to Novo Mundum made him hopeful again." She pressed a hand to her forehead. "God, I hope he's okay." Tears filled her eyes and spilled down her cheeks. She struggled to get herself under control, which only made her sobs turn into racking coughs. "Oh God," she choked out in a sob. "I'm so sorry. . . . I don't . . ."

Keely touched her shoulder. "It's okay. You've been under so much pressure, worried about your father and your brother. Taking care of Diego. Eating those god-awful canned peaches day after day."

Irene let out a laugh and wiped her eyes on the backs of her hands.

"Novo Mundum is going to be great," Keely promised. "All we have to do is get there."

TWENTY-EIGHT

"LOOKS LIKE MOTHER HUBBARD'S KITCHEN," MICHAEL muttered into a bin of empty cans crawling with ants. The moonlight streaming in through the windows showed that the shelves in the luncheonette's kitchen were picked clean, and the walk-in pantry wasn't much better. It had been stupid to hope to find anything worthwhile here. Anyone coming through town would have had the same idea, maybe as long ago as during the evacuation.

Maybe teaming up with Jonah was a bad idea. Clearwater didn't seem very promising, at least not tonight in the dark. Michael wondered again about the friends Jonah had said he was meeting. There was no sign of them, not so far, anyway.

Still, having someone else take on some of Maggie's bottomless need for attention was proving helpful. She was very flirtatious with Jonah, which made Michael wonder if she was trying to make him jealous or was seriously ready to move on to a new boyfriend. Whatever her motive, she was oblivious to the fact that her behavior made Jonah uncomfortable. The first chance Michael had to talk to Jonah alone, he would let the guy know that if he was into Maggie, Michael was cool with it. Not just cool—it would be an enormous relief.

Michael rubbed some of the grime from the counter on his army fatigues. This place hadn't seen life in a long time. Maybe they'd find something in that pharmacy he had spotted across the street.

He was turning around to leave when he heard the sharp click of a weapon being cocked just a few feet away.

"Don't move."

Michael froze, daring to lift only his eyes. It was a girl, her voice unsteady and thin in the darkness. Just a scared teenage girl, but with that gun in her hands, he wasn't going to mess around.

"Do you have a weapon?" she demanded. Only, with her voice shaking, she didn't sound very authoritative.

"No," Michael answered. He slowly held out his hands so she could see they were empty. She swallowed nervously a few times, and Michael wasn't sure if she believed him.

"Are there others patrolling with you?" she asked.

"Patrolling?" Michael repeated. He wasn't sure what

she meant, and rather than give a wrong answer to a freaked-out girl with a gun, he just shook his head in confusion.

The girl cleared her throat. "Have you seen my father?" She pronounced each word carefully despite the tremor in her voice. "I've been looking for my father, Albert Camus."

What the hell? Blood roared in Michael's head, senses on full alert, but another part of his brain clicked into action at the bizarre question. Albert Camus? Wasn't he some kind of famous writer?

He shifted slightly so that he could get a better look at the girl. "Camus was your father?"

She was quivering, her hands shaking as she trained the heavy hunting rifle on him. He swallowed hard. He could smell her fear.

In the dim moonlight all he could make out was a tangle of dark curls and the faint gleam of her eyes. She was little, maybe a few inches over five feet.

What the hell was going on?

"D-don't . . . m-move," she said again, and he stiffened as the gun wavered. "J-just . . . answer m-me." Behind her something creaked, and Michael's heart jolted with fresh panic as she twisted around, swinging the rifle crazily.

It all happened simultaneously: the gunshot, an explosion of plaster dropping onto Michael's head, Jonah shouting "I used to know him! I used to know him!" and Maggie's shriek, echoed by a shriek from the girl with the gun.

Then silence.

The butt of the rifle clattered against the floor as the girl raised a shaking hand to her mouth and stumbled backward. She banged into the counter and stopped.

"We're Novo Mundum," Jonah said, edging toward her. "It's okay."

Novo Mundum? Michael brushed plaster from his hair and face. Apparently the bullet had hit the ceiling above him. *What is Jonah talking about?*

The girl dropped her face into her hands and burst into tears. "Oh God . . . I was so scared. I almost shot you," she added, bewilderment in her voice.

"No kidding," Michael said, feeling his knees sag. The burst of fight-or-flight adrenaline was fading, leaving him weak and a little nauseous.

She turned to face Michael. "It's just—you're wearing a uniform, and my friend was shot by a soldier who looked like you."

"Right." Michael squeezed the lapel of his army jacket. "Guess it's time to rethink my wardrobe."

TWENTY-NINE

KEELY TUGGED THE BLANKET OVER HER SHOULDERS AND crossed her legs, grateful for her new white socks. Although the purple night was giving way to a grey dawn, the apartment remained cool. With all the people in here, you'd think the body heat alone would take the chill off.

People . . . Keely still couldn't believe she was really here, a part of this group of strangers growing bigger every hour, it seemed. First Amber, then Irene and Diego. Now Michael, Maggie, and Jonah were thrown into the mix. She was grateful not to have to face this journey alone, but she wondered how well they would get along.

Oh, well. She yawned and told herself that they weren't

together to make friends, they were together to pool resources and information and to protect one another.

Still, she couldn't quite figure out the new trio: there was definite tension between Maggie and Michael, and Maggie seemed very into Jonah, but he was obviously not her boyfriend. During the long night of exchanging information Keely had been surprised to learn that Maggie and Michael were totally clueless about Novo Mundum, yet Jonah had been recruited.

"I'm going to bed now," Amber announced, stretching.

"Can you just hold off on bed for one more minute?" Keely went to the couch and opened up Amber's laptop. "Let me check and see if Novo Mundum answered. We want to be ready if they're sending a guide this morning."

"Personally, I don't really care about your nouveau community," Maggie said. "I'd like to head over to Memphis or down to Dallas. Back to civilization. My aunt Ruby is in Texas. Anybody else interested?"

Silence fell over them at the thought of going back to that world.

"Civilization isn't what it used to be," Jonah said. "I came from Atlanta, and no matter what happens here, I'm never going back."

Keely pretended to stare at the computer screen, but she listened closely.

"I've got a question, though," Michael said. Keely could tell by the sound of his voice that he was worried. "You three were recruited, but Maggie and I fell into this. If this place is so secret and elite, are they going to take outsiders?"

"I'm sure they'll take me," Amber said. "I mean, if I have information on someone who was already recruited, someone who's a major jerk, they'll want me there instead of him." The words were full of Amber's usual bravado, but Keely was pretty sure she heard a note of fear. Amber wasn't admitting it, but a part of her was obviously worried about whether she'd be accepted at Novo Mundum.

"I wasn't recruited either," Diego said from his wheelchair.

"I think if you're willing to pitch in and make the community work, they'll be happy to have you," Irene said.

"That goes along with what I've heard," Keely added, thinking back to her meeting with Ineo in Griffith Park. "As long as you're open to the group philosophy, there'll be a place for you." She glanced back at the screen as the e-mail page opened. She clicked on the message from Von Moundum. "I got an answer. It's a bunch of numbers and gibberish letters until I decode it, but at least it's an answer."

"Let's see," Jonah said, and everyone moved closer, watching as Keely copied the message to a scrap of paper.

4-1-14-7-5-18 /
XZMMLG HVMW TFRWV
URMW XOFVH
XLNV GL FH
GE 6:17

Reaching under the sofa cushion, Keely slid out the matrix she'd jotted down and nodded at Amber. "I have the text. You can turn it off." They needed to conserve the computer's battery. While Amber closed the laptop, Keely got to work translating the message.

"Okay," Keely said, "the numeric line translates to *danger,* but I don't know what the backslash means."

"Danger?" Amber muttered. "Wow. What a surprise. And here I thought the Big Empty was a giant amusement park."

Michael came behind the couch and read over her shoulder. "A chart. How's that work?"

"A simple cipher," Keely explained. "You can reverse the alphabet so that *A* is *Z,* and *B* is *Y,* and *C* is *X.* Or you can give each letter a numeric equivalent so that *A* is one and *B* is two. Or reverse it so that *A* is 26 and *B* is 25 and so on."

"Huh." Michael nodded. "Cool."

While the others talked, Keely translated the rest of the message.

CANNOT SEND GUIDE
FIND CLUES
COME TO US
TV F:AG

"Or maybe it's *TV U:ZT,*" she muttered, chewing the pencil.

"What's it say?" Diego asked.

"Nothing good." Keely glanced back at the message, checking the decryption. "They're saying, 'Danger, backslash. Cannot send guide. Come to us.' Then this part I can't make out." She passed the paper over to Michael, who gave it a look, then passed it to Diego.

"Oh, great!" Amber threw up her hands. "What good are they if they can't send a guide?"

"What's the danger part about?" Diego said, handing the note to Jonah. "They say danger, but they're not specific."

"Yes, they are." Jonah gazed at the note and then looked up at the group, his dark eyes serious. "The Slash. That's what the backslash means. Danger—the Slash is out there."

A chill seemed to go through the room. The Slash. Keely had heard stories about the renegade group. She shuddered and pulled the blanket tighter around herself.

"So these guys, the Slash, they're as bad as the rumors say?" Irene asked.

Jonah nodded. "They're seriously insane."

"Who are the Slash?" Maggie asked, glancing from Jonah to Michael. Michael shrugged. It was clear this was the first either of them had heard about the group.

"Rebels. Thugs. Crazies," Diego said.

"They have no limits, man," Jonah added. "It's like everything is just some kind of nonstop party—except for them, partying is all about scaring the hell out of people and taking whatever they want, whenever they want it. I just hope they don't . . . I mean, I hope Mickey's okay."

Keely dropped her eyes. She didn't know how to reassure Jonah. Who knew what guys like that would do to a woman?

"So, what, the Slash are all guys?" Maggie piped up.

"Is that why you're worried about your friend? Maybe she's having a great time with them; you never know."

"Maggie," Michael said in a warning tone.

Maggie shrugged. "What? I'm not really getting it—what's so bad about a bunch of guys who just want to have a good time? Be a little crazy? It's not like there's much else worth doing anymore."

"Maggie, these guys sound dangerous," Michael said, an edge to his voice.

"Whatever," Maggie said with a sigh.

"Trust me," Jonah said. Keely could tell he was fighting back anger of his own. "You don't want to run into the Slash, ever. They probably killed my contacts and they probably killed my guide."

"Your guide," Irene repeated. "So the message is telling us that the Slash is the reason our guide can't come help us."

"I'm afraid so," Keely said.

"So how are we supposed to get there?" Jonah said, "when we don't know where *there* is?"

"What about the bottom line?" Keely asked. "TV something? They can't expect us to tune in to a television, can they? To get a message?"

"No way," Diego said. "No TVs left out here. No electricity, either."

"Hold on a second." Jonah squinted at the message. "GE 6:17. What if that's not code? It looks to me like a Bible reference. GE stands for Genesis, the first book in the Old Testament." He looked around. "Anybody got the good book handy?"

Irene's eyes lit up. "Actually, there's one in the apartment upstairs." When the others seemed surprised, she shrugged. "Hey, I had time on my hands. I checked out her bookshelves." She disappeared out the door to retrieve the book.

"Holy crap!" Amber sighed. "Now they're quoting the Bible? They're scaring me. I mean, maybe they're religious weirdos."

"Hey," Jonah snapped. "Just because you read the Bible doesn't make you a weirdo, okay?"

"Okay, whatever, bless me for I have sinned big time." Amber scowled.

Maggie stifled a laugh. She and Amber shared a smirk.

Irene returned with the Bible. Keely sat beside her as she laid it down on the table.

"Okay," Irene said, running her finger down the table of contents. "So let's see . . . Jonah was right. GE *is* Genesis. Genesis, chapter six." She flipped to that section. "Verse fourteen? Here it is: 'Make thee an ark of gopher wood; rooms shalt thou make in the ark, and shalt pitch it within and without with pitch.'"

"It's the story of Noah's Ark," Keely said, trying to absorb it. "But what does it mean?"

"They're telling us to read the Bible, and that's scaring me," Amber said.

"Because they figure we'll be able to find one," Keely told her. "When I was at home, they sent passages from Shakespeare and Greek poets with clues hidden in them. Do you think they're also scary lit freaks?"

Amber crossed her arms, standing her ground. "I still don't like it."

"I just want to know what the message means," Keely said.

"It says to build a boat," Michael declared.

"How are we supposed to do that?" Irene asked, her voice rising in worry. "We don't have tools, lumber—"

Jonah snorted. "You guys are reading way too much into this. A great big lake is right down the street. This is a lakeside community. And you know what that means. Boathouses. Paddleboats. Speedboats. Canoes."

The message reeled through Keely's head. *Come to us. Build a boat.* "Novo Mundum must be on the water," she whispered.

Diego grinned. "The lake is the biggest in the state. Lots of wilderness out there, too. Probably big enough to make a whole community invisible."

That had to be it. "The computer," Keely said to Amber. "I need to get back online . . . say something about water. Ask them if water is the way in." She sat down and scribbled on the pad, trying to come up with a few concise words she could encode.

"So you're saying the message is literal?" Irene asked.

Jonah put a beefy arm over Michael's shoulders and grinned. "I say we get ourselves a boat."

THIRTY

AFTER CATCHING A FEW HOURS OF SLEEP, THE GROUP SPLIT UP TO search for a boat. Irene, Jonah, and Amber went off in one direction; Keely, Michael, and Maggie rode their bikes in the opposite direction. Irene had been reluctant to leave Diego alone in the apartment, but he insisted.

They'd ridden a few miles out of town. Michael had suggested they might have a better chance at finding a working boat away from town, where everything had been picked over.

"I hope the boat we find here is better than that ridiculous canoe you found," Maggie said. "It barely kept us above water."

"It got us out of there," Michael snapped. "And we're still alive—or haven't you noticed?"

"Shush!" Keely held out a hand to make the bickering pair stop. Her senses tingled. She was pretty sure she'd heard a sound.

As the murmur of an engine rose, Keely's heart raced. "Do you hear that?" The brakes on the old bike squealed as she squeezed the handlebars and steered over to the shoulder.

"Someone's coming," Michael said, swinging off his bike and running it into the tall weeds. "Ditch the bikes over here. We need to get out of sight."

"Maybe they can help us," Maggie protested. "Maybe they're our guides!"

"Maggie, just get your butt over here," Michael hissed.

The three of them quickly rolled their bikes behind a clump of thick grasses, then knelt close together. Fighting the rise of fear and adrenaline, Keely huddled down on her elbows.

The vehicle was approaching, its engine growing louder. Keely could see it through the thinnest stalks of grass—a dusty PT Cruiser. A man stood in the skylight, riding like the grand marshal of a parade, scanning the area around him. He had broad shoulders and deeply tanned skin, exposed by his thin, dirty white tank top. His hand gripped a powerful-looking gun that reminded Keely of something Arnold Schwarzenegger would have had in one of his old action movies. Definitely not a weapon regular soldiers or police officers carried around.

Keely swallowed hard when she saw the mark on his face—a purple scar sloping from his chin to his ear. *The Slash.*

As the PT Cruiser sped off in a cloud of dust and gravel, Maggie lifted her head. "Wow," she murmured. "Are those the guys Jonah was talking about?"

Keely stared at her as she nodded. The girl sounded like she was impressed by the thugs. "What do you think they're doing out here?" Keely whispered to Michael.

"Trying to survive, I guess. But I wish they weren't so close to Clearwater."

They stayed in their hiding place until they could no longer hear the rumbling engine. Michael stood and tipped his face up toward the sun. "They're headed east."

"East?" Maggie brushed leaves off her jeans. "Maybe they're going to Memphis. See that? If we were nice to them, we could have hitched a ride."

Keely's jaw fell open.

"Maggie, you do *not* want a lift from those guys," Michael said, his voice even.

"Oh, I don't know," Maggie said in a teasing tone. "There was something kind of sexy about that guy. A girl could feel nice and safe with a man who could seriously take care of himself. And her."

Keely fiddled with her bike, avoiding looking at Michael and Maggie This was clearly a personal fight and had nothing to do with her. Or the Slash, for that matter, she guessed.

"What? Would you really want to get mixed up with the Slash?" Michael demanded.

"Oh, you mean because they have, like, an actual

car, with gas, so they don't have to travel down some river in a crappy boat or ride these stupid bikes?" Maggie sneered. "And they can protect themselves from the trigger-happy cops who want to burn you at the stake for stealing a battery? Yeah, I can see why we want to steer clear of them, all right."

Michael's face darkened. Before they could get into a knock-down, drag-out or say things that they'd never be able to take back, Keely said quickly, "You know, that's a good point. How do you think they got their gas?"

Michael and Maggie both stared at her as if they'd forgotten she was there. She noticed Michael's eyes narrow as he thought over what she'd said.

"Maybe they know how to tap into the reserves at one of the local stations," Michael said. "There's bound to be a small supply left behind. In some of these areas people died or were evacuated within weeks."

"So, does that mean this is their territory?" Keely asked. "Jonah's way station wasn't far from here, right?"

Michael shook his head. "I guess we really have to be more careful."

Keely felt a chill go through her. She had to find a way to get everyone to Novo Mundum, and she had to do it soon.

THIRTY-ONE

IRENE STOOD BESIDE JONAH IN FRONT OF AN ALUMINUM GARAGE door in a house a few blocks from the water. Amber sat, bored, cross-legged on the pavement.

"So what's your big surprise?" she called to them. "I want to go back to the house. This search has been a total bust. Any boat we've found has been total crap!"

"Not total," Irene said with a grin. She turned to Jonah. "Do the honors!"

Jonah gave her a quizzical look, rolled up the garage door, and stepped back.

Through the cloud of dust and dirt a speedboat gleamed like the Holy Grail.

"What do you think?" Irene asked him. "I was surprised

to find it right in the center of the tourist area, but here it is!"

"Let's see." Batting at the circling dust, Jonah stepped into the garage.

He examined the boat from bow to stern. Amazing. It was well cared for . . . serviceable. With some oil and gas he'd have this thing ripping through the water. Life vests, oars, and . . . Was it possible? He climbed up into the helm. "The key's in the ignition," he said with a laugh. "Is this a gift or what?"

Irene's eyes were bright with hope. "Think it'll work?"

"Definitely!" He reached toward her, slapped her five, then hoisted her in the air for a bear hug. "Way to go, Irene."

She laughed, hugging him back.

Jonah felt an unexpected twinge as he held her close, enjoying the warmth of her body against his. Until now he'd thought of Irene as sort of a sister type, and he'd just assumed she and Diego were a thing. But when her pretty eyes looked up at him and those curls straggled into her face . . . it just got him. Maybe there was more between them. Maybe in another time or place they could be together.

A lot of maybes.

"Oh, joy," Amber said flatly, breaking the moment.

Irene glanced over at the girl, then pulled away from Jonah. "Okay, okay. First we have to get this down to the lake and make sure it actually works."

Jonah coughed, trying to shake the fantasies away

and come back down to earth. He tested the boat's trailer. "Sturdy enough. Let me do some work on this here," he said, scanning the garage for tools and oil. "We'll get Michael and the others to help us tow her down later."

"Okay, then." Irene stepped back, tucking a curl behind her ear. "I guess I'll go down to the lake and work on that map again. Unless you need me here."

Jonah squatted under the engine, pretending to check something. He couldn't exactly admit that he did need her. That he just wanted her nearby to . . . have her nearby. "Go on. I've got this covered," he said, never turning around to face her.

THIRTY-TWO

KEELY'S FINGERS WORKED THE PENDANT AT HER NECK AS SHE rounded the stone gate to the cemetery. She wondered if the clue could really be here. Graveyards had always creeped her out in that Stephen King, *Night of the Living Dead* horror way, but ever since she'd helped her mother bury Bree and Dad, it was a whole new kind of hard to walk into one. That was why she'd asked Amber along, although she realized Amber was short on moral support.

She'd gotten another message just a little while ago from Von. It said:

Yes.
ZOZH KLLI BLIRXP
Act VIII, sc. ii

Put your toys back in their proper places when you're done playing.

When she'd applied the reverse cipher, the coded line had translated to ALAS, POOR YORICK. That was from Hamlet—the famous graveyard scene. Was their next clue in a graveyard? It was worth checking out.

"So where's the next message?" Amber paused at the graveyard entrance. "You said it would be here."

"That's what I thought," Keely said. "But we need to find it. It's not going to jump out and bite us."

At least, I hope not, she thought as wind swept brittle leaves around an old grey grave marker.

Amber sat down on a gravestone shaped like an open book. "I'm bored already. What was the clue, anyway?"

Keely unfolded the torn paper where she'd scrawled the message. "The weird part is the citation. Act eight, scene two. There are never eight acts in a Shakespeare play."

"Yeah, so?" Amber muttered. Keely ignored her.

Keely walked past the first line of graves, wondering where to look. The cemetery was smaller than she'd expected—barely the size of a school yard—with names repeated in clusters. HENDERSON. STEELE. COOPER. LEWIS. Gravestones of various colors and ages fanned out in neat rows, though some of the older ones in the back had sunk into the lumpy ground.

Stepping up to the gravestone marked ELIZABETH COOPER, Keely rubbed her necklace thoughtfully. Although Elizabeth had been born in 1907, she'd only survived thirteen years.

Just like Bree. Sometimes Keely forgot that people had lived short lives before Strain 7.

"So what are you looking for?" Amber asked, jolting her back to reality.

Keely sighed. "Well, it might be helpful if someone here was named Hamlet. Or William Shakespeare."

"And then what would you do? Dig up the grave?"

Keely shivered. "I didn't think it that far through. Why don't you help me take a look? I'll start at the back rows; you do this side," she said, heading along the stone fence to the rear of the cemetery. "Look for a weird name or maybe someone who was born or died on August second."

"Why that date?" Amber asked.

"Act eight, scene two. Eight two, August second."

As Keely moved past the stones, she tried to avoid reading the personal inscriptions and mentally calculating the ages of the dead. Better not to know the personal details of the people in the graves marked EMILY JAMESON or JACOB MYERS.

Across the cemetery Amber was calling out names in a bored voice. "David Wethers. Mildred Wethers. Zane Porter. William Shakespeare."

"What?" Keely paused at a peach marble memorial.

"Just kidding."

When the two girls met in the middle, Amber shrugged. "Nothing. What next?"

"I don't know." Keely glanced over the tombstone grid. Ten rows, six across. Sixty graves.

Act 8, scene 2.

What if the clue was referencing the grid layout of the cemetery? So what would 8 2 mean? Eighth row, second grave in?

Could it be that simple?

Quickly she moved to the eighth row. The second grave from the left wall—marked JOSEPH NEWBURG—was one of the few that had a bouquet of flowers on it. He was born June 12, 1943, died May 3, 2003. Keely ran her hand over the tombstone as she stared at the inscription. Was there some significance in the numbers? An anagram in the name?

"What? What do you see?" Amber came over, frowning at the grave as Keely explained her logic.

"These fake flowers are so tacky," Amber said, nudging the plastic vase with the toe of her boot. It toppled over, rolling on the smooth stone. "My mother used to keep adding them to my grandfather's grave. Bunches of silk roses and plastic mums."

"Sounds like your mother liked them," Keely said. "Did you put some on her grave?"

Amber squatted down to pick up the runaway flowers. "There was no grave. No money for any of that. Her body was picked up by the DU."

Keely felt a wave of pity. She could still picture the Decontamination Unit with their black vans, sweeping through neighborhoods day and night, collecting dead bodies. It was a point of pride not to need them, to have the money to arrange a private decontamination and burial. Of course, toward the end almost everyone was picked up by the DU, when life—and death—became so crazy that there were too many funerals to keep track of.

She went back to concentrating on the clue. "Okay, Mr. Newburg, what am I looking for?" Keely mused, walking around his shiny marble headstone.

"I think he just answered you," Amber said, poking her finger into the empty flower vase.

"What?" Keely asked, but Amber was already sliding a piece of paper out of the green plastic cylinder and unfolding it. "A message in the flowerpot, and it's all those jumbled letters that Novo Mundum likes to use." She handed the note up to Keely, grinning. "Mr. Newburg just gave us the message."

THIRTY-THREE

MICHAEL TRIED TO IGNORE THE GNAWING HUNGER IN HIS GUT AS he stood back on the dock and nodded to Jonah. "Let her rip." They'd been working on the boat for hours, ever since they dragged it out of the house and down into the water. Michael had assigned jobs to the others; then he and Jonah went to work. In the next minute they'd find out if all those hours had been worth anything.

His jaw clenched in determination, Jonah pushed the ignition button on the boat's dashboard. The engine roared to life in a cloud of dense black smoke.

Success! "Whoo-hoo!" Michael shouted, pumping his fist in the air and clapping Jonah on the back. "Yes! We now have a mode of transportation."

"Excellent!" Jonah's head bobbed with satisfaction.

Suddenly Michael frowned. "Cut it off," he ordered.

"What?" Jonah asked.

Michael reached past him and switched the key in the ignition. The motor abruptly shut down.

"What's the matter, man?" Jonah asked.

Michael shook his head. "We're so stupid," he moaned. He looked at Jonah. "The noise. It carries for miles on the water. We may have just attracted soldiers, renegades, and rebels from every neighboring county."

Jonah smacked his head. "You know, for two bright guys, we just did a seriously dumb thing."

"Not to mention wasting several hours slaving over this piece of machinery getting it to work," Michael added, "when we're never going to be able to use it."

"Well, at least we know we can if we have to," Jonah said.

"So do we have oars in this thing?" Michael asked.

"I guess that's next on our list to find," Jonah said.

"Found the next clue!" Keely called as she dashed down the dock. Amber trailed behind her. "The graveyard paid off!"

"Too bad you don't know what the message says," Amber grumbled.

"Not yet," Keely countered. Michael could tell that Keely was too pleased to let even Amber's permanent negativity get to her.

Irene came out from behind some tall weeds and flopped down on the dock at Keely's feet. "I'm tired," she declared.

"How did it go?" Michael asked her. He had asked

Irene to try to start making a map of the immediate shoreline. He'd hate to be trying to make a getaway only to run aground on some boulders or surprise shallows.

Irene sighed. "Pretty well, though I didn't get very far. It got too dark to see." She laughed. "And I got too hungry. I wonder what Maggie has managed to wrangle for dinner."

"So this is where you all are," Maggie said, appearing around the corner of the boathouse as if Irene had conjured her simply by mentioning her name.

"Is dinner ready?" Michael asked.

"Um, well, that's why I'm here," Maggie said. She flashed a bright smile. "Just wondering if anyone has any suggestions on what I should make. Or if anyone wants to help. I'm not much of a cook."

Michael felt his temper start to boil up again, and he wasn't sure he could hold it back much longer. "Everyone's got something to do," he said. "And dinner was your assignment. You were supposed to figure it out."

Maggie snorted. "You and your assignments," she said.

"Yeah, did I miss the part where you were elected president of the Big Empty?" Amber added, backing up Maggie. "I guess you kind of took the job the same way MacCauley did."

"What are you going to do, Michael? Sentence me to execution because I didn't collect a couple of cans of beans?" Maggie drawled sarcastically. Amber laughed.

"That's it!" Michael exploded. "I've had it with you."

Maggie shook her head. "You've had it with *me?* News flash, buddy: I'm sick to death of your holier-than-thou, boss-of-the-world act. What, I'm supposed to be all grateful because you brought me out to the middle of nowhere?"

"You should be grateful I didn't leave you to fend for yourself back in New York." Now that he had started, Michael couldn't stop. All the rage and frustration spewed out of him. "I ruined my life for you. I didn't have to do that. Don't you get that? My life is over—because of you." He started laughing, a hard, angry laugh. "And the worst part of all? I was on my way to meet you so that I could dump you."

He could see Maggie's shocked expression and the stunned faces surrounding them, but he didn't care. He stepped right up to her. "That's right," he said, his voice low. "I was on my way to break up with you. Instead I got stuck with you."

Maggie's face went from hurt to hard in record time. "Go to hell," she said. She spun around and stomped off the dock

"I don't have to go there," Michael called after her. "I'm already there, thanks to you. If you don't want to be here, fine. Go run after that sexy Slash dude if you think that's an improvement."

He watched her vanish around the corner. He shook his head and then noticed everyone standing there, staring at him.

"Don't we have things to do?" he demanded. Then he stalked off the boat, and in the opposite direction from Maggie.

THIRTY-FOUR

"WHAT BUG FLEW UP HIS ASS?" AMBER ASKED MAGGIE AS SHE caught up to the furious girl on her way back to the apartment.

"You know what? I am done with this . . . this little Power Rangers team." Maggie stormed inside, Amber on her heels. "Michael's right. It's time for me to take off."

Was Maggie actually serious about leaving? It sure seemed like it. So what did that mean for her?

"How about you?" Maggie asked, as if guessing her thoughts. "You want to come along, or are you going to stick with the tyrant?"

Amber couldn't help feeling a twinge of satisfaction picturing the expression on Keely's face when she heard that Amber and Maggie took off. That would teach her not to be all lecture girl with Amber, acting like Amber wasn't capable of taking care of herself.

But there was still Novo Mundum and Carter. . . .

Yeah, well, you already know one of them doesn't want you, Amber told herself. *And there's a good chance Novo Mundum won't either.* The truth was, even if Michael and Keely and the others actually found this secret place, Amber wasn't so convinced that they'd really open their doors to everyone who wasn't invited. What if they didn't believe her about Carter? Or didn't care? At least if she stuck with Maggie, she'd have someone around who didn't bug her . . . too much.

"Why not?" Amber said, flashing Maggie a smile. "Let's go for it. I'll even leave a note for Keely to have fun deciphering."

THIRTY-FIVE

"I CAN'T BELIEVE SHE'D DO THIS." KEELY MUTTERED THE thought out loud even though she was alone in the apartment, except for Diego sleeping on the couch. Irene had said it wasn't a good idea to move him at this stage, and it was easier to elevate his leg on the arm of the couch than to keep it propped on pillows in bed.

Keely stared down at the clue from the graveyard. It translated as a list of famous people that meant nothing to her. She couldn't make it make sense.

She fingered her necklace, feeling overwhelmed by a sense of helplessness. She just couldn't wrap her mind around the fact that Amber had really taken off. Not only taken off, but left them stranded. She had taken her laptop with her, which meant no more messages from Novo Mundum.

Keely hoped that this was some kind of silly temper tantrum and that Amber and Maggie would come back—without soldiers or members of the Slash right behind them, holding guns to their heads. Keely blinked, trying to force the awful image out of her head. Amber wasn't as tough as she liked to act, but she did have street smarts, Keely reassured herself. The same could not be said of Maggie. She could be a real liability for Amber.

Diego shifted and groaned on the couch.

"Wish you could help me," Keely whispered, glancing over at him, then back down at the list that defied decoding.

"Irene?" Diego rasped.

"It's Keely." She stood and sat beside him, holding out a cup of water. "Do you want a drink?"

He opened his eyes, obviously focusing, though they shimmered with the glassy look of fever. "Thanks, Keely." He took a sip. "What's got you all hopped up?"

She paused. There was no point in telling him about their setback or the fact that Amber and Maggie were MIA. She decided to focus on the other obstacle of the moment. "It's another message from Novo Mundum. In code again." She handed him the list. "I was hoping for a map, but instead I got this bizarro party list."

Diego stared at it, blinked, then sighed. "Man, it's all swimming."

"Same for me," she said. "Try figuring out how Oprah

Winfrey relates to Michelangelo relates to Christian Dior. It's like playing Six Degrees of Kevin Bacon."

"I can't. . . ." Diego squinted at it. "Man, I can't even see the small letters. Just the big ones, down, like a crossword puzzle."

"Huh?" Keely knelt beside the couch for a closer look.

"When you read the capital letters down. See. It says MAP. And what's the second one? COBBLER." He let out a breath and dropped the paper to his lap, closing his eyes.

But Keely's pulse was picking up in excitement. "Diego, I think you have something there." She picked up the paper and read the first letter down.

INITIAL LIST FOR WELCOME PARTY
Michelangelo
Anton Chekov
Patrick Henry

Christian Dior
Oprah Winfrey
Bob Barker
Bill Clinton
Lawrence Fishburne
Ellen DeGeneres
Robert Frost

She saw it now. MAP COBBLER. There was a map at Tom-the-Cobbler's—the shoe repair shop. It had to be.

"Diego, you did it! This must be it!" She grabbed her red hunting jacket, then banged out the door and ran into the night, toward the house with the shoe sign mounted in the front.

Her heart beat double time and every beat thudded: *A map. A map. A map.*

THIRTY-SIX

As Amber's bicycle wobbled over a rut in the road, she sucked in a deep breath of freedom. It felt good to be out on her own again, doing whatever she wanted, not listening to anyone.

"So . . . where should we go?" Maggie asked as she cruised alongside Amber through the deserted little town a few miles from Clearwater.

"I don't know." Amber hadn't really thought about going somewhere in particular. Right now she was just enjoying the feel of the wind on her face, the stars in the night sky overhead.

"I was thinking we could head toward a city, like Memphis or Dallas," Maggie said. "Maybe we could sneak onto a ghost train, like what you and Keely did.

No way am I going to pedal a gazillion miles on this hunk of rust."

"I guess," Amber said. She wasn't sure what they should do, really. Luckily the morning sickness had passed, but she was going to have to worry about what was going on in her body at some point.

Finding Carter and trashing him in front of everyone had been as far as her plan had gone. But the thing was, she'd been starting to think maybe this Novo Mundum place wouldn't have been so terrible for her—or for the baby. So had she made a major mistake leaving Keely and the others, if they actually did find the way in?

That still wouldn't mean they'd let me stay there, she reminded herself. No, heading off on her own with Maggie was the right thing to do. If they could keep themselves safe, that was.

Suddenly Amber's ears picked up a new sound in the night—the hum of an engine. Turning toward the road, she saw the glow of lights. "Someone's coming! Get out of sight. Over here!" She dragged her bike to the side of a woodshed and motioned to Maggie.

"Good." Maggie climbed off her bike and walked it over beside Amber's. "Maybe they can give us a ride."

Amber tugged Maggie's jeans to get the girl to duck down behind the woodpile. She squinted at the lights as they passed the roadside trees. An olive green truck. The top was off in the back, and men hung from the metal ribs that were usually covered with a tarp, their rifles swinging casually as the truck turned up the driveway.

"Soldiers," Amber whispered. They were coming their way.

Alarm shot through her, and she felt sweat beading on her forehead despite the cool night. *Are they following us? What do I tell them?* She fought back her panic. *I can talk my way out of this if I need to,* she assured herself. *I've been in worse spots before, right?*

Maggie poked her head up. "What are they doing out here?"

"Hide!" Amber hissed, yanking Maggie back. "And play it smart. Remember what those guys did to Diego? If you want to stay alive, keep your mouth shut!"

Maggie folded into the hiding spot next to Amber. Amber squeezed herself as small as she could, trying to ignore the trembling in her knees. Peering through the space between two split logs, she watched the truck chug past the woodshed, past the garage. Its brakes screeched; then the driver put it in reverse and rammed it toward the back of a pale green house.

Was the little house one of the soldiers' headquarters?

With all the places to choose from in the Big Empty, it didn't seem likely. And as the soldiers piled out, they didn't head inside. Instead they scrambled to a spot beside the back porch.

"This one's nearly empty," one of the soldiers said, shifting the propane tank. "But we might as well take it. They can decide what to do with it."

Already two other guys in fatigues were at work, one unscrewing the fittings on the tank, the other lowering the tailgate of the truck.

The propane. They were taking the tank. Now Amber realized that the other tall forms in the truck—which she'd mistaken for a dozen soldiers—were actually propane tanks. They were collecting propane tanks.

"Is this it for tonight?" one of the soldiers asked.

"We got orders for a bunch of places," the guy in charge answered. "The last one is Clearwater."

Clearwater? Amber felt the air catch in her throat. They were going to collect tanks from Clearwater tonight.

"What's the big hurry?" a soldier asked as he wiggled the propane tank away from the fittings. "Where's this stuff going?"

"I don't know, Kansas City? Maybe even D.C. Don't you know, brother? This stuff is liquid gold. It's fuel, man. Whoever controls it controls the roads. We want to make sure that's us, not the psychos out here."

"Help me get this in the truck."

As the soldiers slid the tank up a makeshift ramp, Amber couldn't stop thinking about Keely back in Clearwater. Diego, a decent guy who couldn't walk. Would they have taken the usual precautions, or would the soldiers see signs of life? As careful as everyone had been, they'd still been taking risks, necessary risks to work on getting to Novo Mundum. If these soldiers had any kind of brains, they'd realize people were there.

Five people, to be exact, sleeping in a little apartment behind the post office. Sitting ducks.

THIRTY-SEVEN

KEELY WAS RUNNING DOWN THE STREET TO TOM-THE-Cobbler's when she saw Michael striding toward her. It was so dark, they nearly banged into each other. She stopped, gulping to catch her breath. "Hey," she said. "I'm onto another clue—Diego helped me piece that list together. I think they left us a map!"

"That's great," he said. "Let's hope you're right." He held up a large compass. "I think this will help us navigate." Then he looked down at his feet. "So, is anything else . . . Things are all still the same otherwise?"

Keely winced, realizing how worried he was about Maggie, even if he wasn't admitting it. When Jonah had told Keely, Michael, and Irene about Amber's note, Michael hadn't said a word, but Keely had seen the frustration all over his face. "They're not back yet," Keely said softly. "But I'm sure they will be." She wasn't, but what else could she say?

"Yeah, well, as soon as we know where we're going, we leave, whether they're back or not," he said. Keely didn't think his tone sounded quite as definite as his words. It was obvious Michael still felt responsible for Maggie, just as Keely did for Amber.

"I'll see you back at the apartment," she said. "I'm going to go check out this clue."

"Good luck."

Keely lit a candle once she got inside the little shop. On the far wall sat pairs of discarded shoes, most of them useless dress shoes, all of them pillaged by passing travelers. Amber had been in the other day and scrounged a pair of boots.

Keely went over to search the shelves. What if Amber and Maggie really didn't come back in time? Keely hated the idea of leaving Amber behind, especially knowing the truth about her condition. But was she really going to sacrifice everything she'd worked so hard for for someone who didn't even seem to want her friendship?

The shoes were empty, as were the flimsy clip-on-bracket shelves. Keely held the candle up, searching the tiny room for a hiding place. A place with permanence. Something that wouldn't be moved.

Under the carpet? She nudged a corner of the rug with her toe. It looked new and seemed to be stapled down. The two plastic chairs? The tools? The workbench, with its worn surface and thick wooden supports? She gave the worktable a nudge—solid. It would be difficult to move from this space. That had to be it.

Lowering the candle to the floor, Keely ran her fingertips against the underside of the table until they came to a square of paper. Sticky, probably glued up there. With one tug she ripped it off. It was a manila envelope. She tore it open and her eyes lit up.

A map. It was a map of the lake, And on this map there was a beautiful, gorgeous, glorious X. Marking the spot!

Keely slid to the floor, relief, gratitude, and joy washing over her. "I found it," she whispered.

She looked at the map again and saw that there was a message written on the corner of the map:

Welcome to our nation's capital! Looking forward to seeing you at the white tree. Carve the right name into the bark and the welcoming committee will greet you.

She clutched the map to her chest, shaking.
The ticket to Novo Mundum was in her hands

THIRTY-EIGHT

AMBER CROUCHED LOWER AS THE TRUCK'S LIGHTS FLASHED over the woodpile, then bounced away down the driveway to the road. Only when she could barely hear the engine anymore did she stand, slowly. She brushed the dirt off her jeans, realizing her hands were trembling.

Maggie stood next to her. "Well, I'm glad they're gone," she said. Her voice had its usual careless tone, but Amber could hear a hint of something new—actual fear, for once. "Do you want to see what's inside the house or just head on?" Maggie added. "Maybe we should use their bathroom while we have the chance."

Amber squinted at Maggie. "Are you kidding me?" she said. "Did you hear what those guys said? They're headed to Clearwater. As in, where everyone else is probably sleeping all cozily, no clue they're about to be in serious trouble. Maggie, we have to find a way to warn them."

Maggie avoided her gaze. "Look, it's not like I want something bad to happen to them. But come on, do you really want us to risk our own lives to save them? Do you think they'd do that for *us*?"

Um, didn't Michael do exactly that? Amber thought. He was a pompous jerk, yes, and Amber would much rather never see his face again. But he had dropped his whole life for Maggie—and it turned out he wasn't even into her anymore. Keely had done the same thing for her, putting herself out there in spite of the risks. Amber couldn't sit back and let them get annihilated.

She slid off her backpack, then reluctantly took the other pack with the computer out of the basket of the bike. She hated leaving her stuff behind, but she'd move faster without the weight.

"What are you doing?" Maggie demanded. "Don't tell me you're serious. You're really going back? Amber, this is crazy. There's no way you'll get there before the soldiers."

"Oh yeah? The truck has to go other places first."

"You'll get yourself killed," Maggie insisted.

"That sounds like a dare, and I like dares." She grinned at Maggie. "Come on, let's go."

But Maggie folded her arms, standing her ground. "No. I'm not going back"

Amber gaped at her. "You're going to travel through the Big Empty alone? You?"

Maggie's eyes flashed with anger, then she smiled.

"I'm a little more capable than people think. I'll take my chances."

Amber paused, wondering what was up with that. Did Maggie maybe have more of a plan than she was sharing with Amber? Or maybe Maggie just *played* damsel in distress so that she wouldn't have to be responsible and could get guys to do stuff for her.

Whatever. Amber didn't have time to figure out Maggie's story. She had to make sure those soldiers didn't finish what they'd started with Diego.

"Okay, then." Amber stood on the pedal of her bike and cruised up the drive. "You can keep my laptop," she called back over her shoulder. "Good luck."

"Yeah, you too," Maggie called as Amber hit the paved road and began pumping the pedals.

Clenching her fingers around the handlebars, Amber worked her legs until the bike was speeding down the road. This was going to be one serious workout, but pregnant girls didn't have to put up their feet and eat nachos all day, right?

The bike hit a bump and she struggled to maintain balance. She could do this. She could beat the truck. She had to.

THIRTY-NINE

We are almost there, Keely thought as she headed to the dock. *So close.*

She had replaced the clue in the graveyard. She figured that was what Von had meant by "Put your toys back in their proper places when you're done playing." Leave the clues for the next seeker to find. But she hadn't replaced the map yet. She wanted to show it to the others first.

Reaching the path, Keely broke into a jog. Suddenly she felt lighter, the closest to happy she'd imagined she could feel. She hurried down the dock and leapt into the boat, where the others were waiting.

"Hey, guys," she called as her sneakers scraped against the wood. "Success! I cracked the final clue."

Michael's face eased with relief. "That's great. Found a route?"

"A location and the official handshake! Look at this." Keely lowered the map to their light, and they huddled around it.

A sound caught Keely's attention. She turned around, but all she saw were the weeds. She listened and thought she could make out the sound of a voice. Or maybe it was just the wind.

"What was that?" Jonah asked.

Michael cocked his head. "I heard it too."

Keely was staring at the weeds when Amber's head appeared. Her cheeks were red, her hair blowing back as she bounced down the path on a bike. "Hey!"

Keely felt an intense wave of relief.

"I told you they'd come back," Jonah said.

"Where's Maggie?" Michael asked, peering behind Amber.

Amber dropped the bike and stumbled toward them, obviously struggling to catch her breath. "She's not here," she finally got out. "But you'd better get moving, all of you. There's a truckload of soldiers on the way. We saw them collecting propane tanks and one of them mentioned that they're headed toward Clearwater."

Michael's face hardened. He swung toward Jonah. "We ready to go?"

Jonah nodded. "We're good. I'll take a last check while you guys get our stuff."

"There's no time to pack!" Amber warned.

"She's right," Michael said. "But we have to get Diego down here. Irene, can you handle that?"

Irene was already on her feet, backing toward the path. "I'll need help getting him into the wheelchair. He's too weak."

"Right behind you," Michael said, climbing from the boat to the dock. "Keely . . . the map. Talk Jonah through the route we need to take while we're getting Diego."

"Wait—what about Maggie?" Keely blurted.

Amber's face clouded over, and she met Keely's gaze with a look that said it all. "She's not coming," she said softly.

Keely's eyes widened. Maggie had stayed behind, even knowing the group was about to be ambushed by soldiers.

But not Amber. The girl who had practically ordered a printed announcement stating she was only out for herself had hightailed it back to Clearwater to warn Keely, and the others, that they were in danger. Maybe Amber cared a little more than she wanted to admit. And maybe that meant a little more to Keely than *she* wanted to admit.

Michael glanced from Amber to Keely, a look of defeat in his eyes. "She made the choice, she has to live with it." With that, he ran up the dock after Irene.

FORTY

IRENE'S HEART BROKE AT THE SIGHT OF DIEGO ON THE SOFA. IN pain, pale, weak, almost delirious. It would be a miracle if he survived this final part of the trip.

"Diego! Wake up. We're going to Novo Mundum." As Irene spoke, she moved the wheelchair beside him and eased his leg down from the sofa's armrest.

"Huh? Oh." Diego moaned. "Okay."

Michael got into position behind Diego, clasping him under the arms. "You ready? One, two, three."

On three they both lifted. It tortured Irene to move Diego's leg at all, but she clenched her teeth and helped him bend his knees, tucking his feet onto the ledge of the wheelchair. She placed a folded blanket over him, then pushed the chair toward the door.

"I know it hurts," she whispered as they hurried toward the dock. "I know, but this is the only way. You'll have real help soon. We're really close now." They were on the road now, not as smooth as Irene would have liked, but at least it was paved. How long would it take them to get to the lake? It was a short trip, five or ten minutes. . . .

"Hear that rumble? It's a truck. We've got to move faster," Michael said, running alongside her. "Do you want me to push?"

"No, I can do it," Irene told him as she stepped up the pace. She was almost running, wincing for Diego's pain every time she hit a bump. The only problem was, moving so quickly, she didn't have time to avoid pocks in the road.

As they passed the shoe repair shop, Keely popped out the door and joined them. "I replaced the map," she said. "Clearwater is ready for the next group of Novo Mundum seekers."

"Good luck to them," Irene said breathlessly. "Come on, we have to hurry."

When they reached the dock, Amber was waiting, urging them on toward the boat. "I saw some lights through the trees," she said. "I think the soldiers are nearby."

As carefully as possible Irene, Michael, and Keely struggled to get Diego from the chair into the boat without hurting his leg. Then the three of them climbed on board themselves, and Amber came on last, dragging the folded-up wheelchair in with her.

"Look out, everybody!" she hissed as she scrunched in between Keely and Michael. "Duck!"

Irene dropped down, her hands hitting the floor-boards as a beam of light shot over them.

FORTY-ONE

THIS IS EXCRUCIATING, KEELY THOUGHT AS SHE HUDDLED nervously against the side of the boat. Every one of her muscles ached as she and the others lay hidden in the bottom of the boat, waiting for the soldiers to leave the area. After some time Michael had stealthily unhitched them from the dock to allow the boat to drift away from shore. But they still couldn't risk getting up and being seen. Not yet.

She tried to distract herself by gazing up at the sky, the grey, frothy clouds filtering the moon. Somewhere, under that same moon, Novo Mundum waited for them.

"Okay," Michael whispered, lifting his head. "I think we're covered by those trees. Let's paddle from here."

Everyone shifted as Jonah and Michael went to

either side of the boat and dropped in the paddles. Keely glanced behind them for any sign of the soldiers, but she couldn't see the dock. They'd escaped undetected. So far.

"How about some navigation?" Michael said. "Anything look familiar?"

"We need to get past that spit of land to the north," Keely said, moving closer to the helm. Keeping their heads down, Keely and Irene gave directions as the paddles dipped quietly into the water.

Minutes stretched on, the quiet torturously punctuated by croaking frogs. It took a solid hour to cross the lake, but at least the soldiers seemed not to have noticed them and had moved on.

"We're moving into a narrow part of the lake, getting close to the beach with the tree," Keely said. "Watch out on your right. What's ahead?"

Jonah shoved his paddle in to steer left, squinting over the windshield. "Looks like boulders on the right."

"Stop paddling," Irene said.

The splash of the paddles gave way to the call of a loon. Crickets' songs. The lapping of water against the wall of the boat.

Keely could see it now—a barren strip of beach and beyond it, thick woods.

Birch woods. White trees.

"That's it," she said.

They paddled again, this time with urgency. As the hull of the boat scraped against the bottom, Michael, Jonah, Amber, Irene, and Keely clambered out and dragged the boat ashore. Together they all lowered Diego and his wheelchair onto the sand.

"Now what?" Amber asked.

Keely scanned the beach. A white tree? There were dozens. Then she spotted a tall dead tree trunk, its bleached white wood gleaming in the moonlight at the edge of the clearing. She hurried and saw dozens of names carved into it. KAREN + JASON 4EVER. PATRICK WUZ HERE. DON VUMMUN.

DON VUMMUN? That was a familiar group of letters. . . .

Her excitement mounted. "The knife," she said.

Jonah stepped up beside her and handed her his knife.

Keely held up the knife, then halted, biting her lower lip. "The map said 'carve the right name.' It's the final test. If I carve the wrong name . . ."

"Novo Mundum?" Amber asked.

"That seems too obvious," Irene objected.

"Not Novo Mundum," Keely said. "Von Moundum."

"What's that?" Irene asked.

"An anagram for Novo Mundum." Carefully Keely carved the name into the trunk of the tree. "And the name of my pen pal."

When she was done, she sank back onto her heels. Nothing. Could she have been wrong?

"They didn't know when to expect us," Michael said. "They probably have to get someone out here on short notice."

Keely nodded, trying to keep breathing.

A rustling movement in the trees made her heart

pound louder. Two hooded, cloaked figures stepped out from the woods and approached them. Keely stood up, her legs trembling.

Just a few feet from the group the two removed their hoods. A pretty red-haired girl about Keely's age and a guy in his twenties smiled at them.

"Sorry about the cloak-and-dagger," the guy said. "We just have to be sure."

"I'm Liza," the girl said. "This is Gabe." She nodded toward the young man. "Welcome to Novo Mundum."

Beside her, Irene was sobbing. Jonah had his eyes shut, a beatific smile on his face. Diego's eyes glittered with awe from his spot in the wheelchair. Amber's mouth had dropped open in shock. Michael kept looking from Gabe to Liza, his head bobbing.

Keely felt faint—with exhaustion, with relief, with the terror of the last weeks. But underneath all that, she also finally felt hope.

Novo Mundum.

I found my future.